"Miss Callahan?" Noah called, respond.

"Kate?" he tried again, all too aware he'd used her given name.

A soft moan escaped her lips and he closed his eyes in gratitude that she hadn't gotten herself killed.

"I'm all right," she finally said with a groggy tone as she attempted to sit up on her own.

Noah placed a hand in the small of her back to keep her from falling backward, her proximity wreaking havoc on his senses.

After a moment, she made a move to stand, but quickly sat back down again, amongst the piles of splintered wood.

"Maybe I'll just sit here a moment and lick my wounded pride."

Noah laughed. *She'll be just fine.*

"Let's get you inside," he said, holding out his hand to her. "The air is a might chilly tonight."

When her fingers touched his, a light, tingling jolt spread up his arm, but he couldn't pull away. He attempted to help her to her feet, but her legs buckled beneath her.

"Upsi-daisy," he said, her hand still firm in his grasp.

Kate started to giggle, but winced in pain.

"I think I may have hurt a little more than my pride," she said, rubbing her ankle.

Without waiting any longer, Noah released her hand and reached down, scooping her up easily into his arms. He climbed the porch stairs, opened the door, and carried her inside.

"Where are your quarters?" he asked, unable to keep the obvious rasp from his voice.

She turned toward him, her hand resting at the button of his shirt, her face so close to his he could feel her breath on his lips. He looked down into her wide, trusting eyes.

Big mistake.

NOAH

DEARDON MINI-SERIES, BOOK THREE

KELLI ANN MORGAN

inspire books

Inspire Books
A Division of Inspire Creative Services
937 West 1350 North, Clinton, Utah 84015, USA

NOAH

An Inspire Book published by arrangement with the author
First Inspire Books paperback edition September 2015

ISBN-13: 978-1-939049-21-6
ISBN-10: 1939049210

Printed in the United States of America

PRAISE FOR THE NOVELS OF BESTSELLING AUTHOR

KELLI ANN MORGAN

"This story could have flowed from the pens of the masters; Max Brand, Zane Grey or Louis L'Amour. These greats have stood alone for decades upon an acme seldom reached or yet to be passed by others that have tried. Kelli Ann Morgan has done the unthinkable and written a story that is equal or better than those western-writing icons of the past."

—Thom Swennes on THE RANCHER

"Kelli Ann is a word seamstress and a master at the trade…"

—Book Lovin' Freak on LUCAS

"Kelli Ann knows how to write a charming hero you can't help but fall in love with."

—American Girl on LUCAS

"Kelli Ann Morgan writes the most loveable male characters that I know!"

—C. Patterson on LUCAS

"I love mail-order bride books. It speaks to me of women with great strength and courage to travel and marry a stranger. This story is so special that I read it in one day. It definitely is a book to read any day of the week or season. It had just the right balance of romance and intrigue. It was something believable. Ms. Kelli Ann Morgan is an excellent story teller."

—Linda M. on JONAH

ACKNOWLEDGEMENTS

To Dean Wesley Smith, for your encouraging words of inspiration and the reminder that writing is supposed to be as fun and exciting for me as it is for my readers. Your ideas and suggestions were a real game-changer for me and have made all the difference.

To my wonderful copy editor and beta readers, Rocky Palmer, Darcy Fairbanks, and Brad Asay—your role in the process has been invaluable to me. I so appreciate all the time and energy that you spent in helping me to make this book its best.

To Brett Dawson, for your additional insights on the inner-workings, animal behaviors, and seasons on a cattle ranch.

To CharlesVanHeule at the Laramie Historic Railroad Depot, for taking the time to help me research the weather data for that first winter after the railroad went through Laramie.

And to my alpha reader and sounding board, Grant—your brutal honesty, constructive criticism, and encouragement are instrumental in helping me create the kinds of stories that others like to read. Thank you for your love and support. I am one lucky woman to be your wife!

To my son, Noah,
who couldn't wait for one of my
characters to be his namesake.
I love you, kiddo, and am so proud of you.

NOAH

DEARDON MINI-SERIES, BOOK THREE

CHAPTER ONE

Laramie, Wyoming Territory, September 1868

"Step away!"

Kate Callahan had never heard her father's voice shake with such scarcely veiled ire.

Deputy Marshal "Big" Steve Long threw his head back and laughed with dark amusement as he swung down off his horse. His long, dusty coat flapped behind him in the light autumn breeze. When his steel-like eyes met her father's, his expression had grown cold. A snarl rested on his lips.

"You got nerve, Emmett, I'll give you that. How 'bout we give you some time to think on it? It's a might generous offer under the circumstances."

"No need to wait, Long. I won't be changing my mind."

The crooked lawman scowled, his thick, brown moustache twitching with the movement.

Her father moved his hand to his hip, rubbing the edge of his holster. "This ranch rightfully belongs to me and my daughter. It is our home and I will not sign it over to you or any other common thug who may come our way."

Kate held her breath. She'd already lost her mother and two brothers to the fever. She couldn't lose him too. With as much courage as she could muster, she stepped out from beneath the tree branch where her father had instructed she wait, and walked forward, linking her arm with his.

Twelve dead ranchers, maybe more, had already lost their lives after refusing the short-tempered marshal. Kate had to make sure there was no excuse for the deputy to draw his weapon.

"The marshal's just trying to be a helpful neighbor, Da. There are a lot of ranchers having a hard time of it this fall."

"You should listen to your daughter, Emmett. Pretty and smart." He winked at her.

Kate's skin crawled at his appraisal.

"We're just trying to help." He tugged his belt up higher on his waist, the light glinting off one of the metal bullets that rested there, and sniffed.

Bile rose up in the back of Kate's throat. His conniving arrogance, coupled with his putrid stench, filled her with indignation and disgust.

"We don't need the kind of help you're offering," her father said. "Now, I've got work to do." He raised a challenging brow.

The marshal stared at him a moment longer, spit in the dirt, then tipped his hat and returned to his mount. Before climbing up into the saddle, he turned back to them.

"We'll be back for a visit." The threat hung on the air like draped laundry.

Kate shuddered, the hairs of her arms standing on end. He may have come alone this time, but when he returned, it would be with his half-brothers, Ace and Con Moyer—the so-called marshal and justice of the peace.

The Callahans had only been in Laramie for just over a year, coming on invitation from a Mr. Levi Redbourne, a representative for the Union Pacific Railroad. Their stead had been one of the first erected and was far and away the largest and most elaborate of all the ranches around town—next to their neighbors', Nathanial and Mary Boswell.

Kate tried to push the worry of what the three brutes might do when they returned to confront her father. She had to be strong. For his sake. She tightened her hold on her da's arm, pulling herself closer to him.

"We'll be waiting," her father replied in whispered tones that only she could hear.

They stood, unmoving, under the grand wooden archway, watching the marshal until he vanished from their sight.

Her father patted her hand. "I best be getting' back to work. The cattle aren't going to tend to themselves and we've got a few downed fences that need mending." He turned and strode toward the barn. "And, Katie darlin', don't be forgettin' your cooking lesson," he called back over his shoulder.

Kate groaned.

She glanced at the place where the marshal had disappeared, shook the anxious thoughts from her head, then turned back for the main house.

Although, Fannie, the family's cook, would be teaching her how to make her flakey butter biscuits today, the kitchen was the last place Kate wanted to be. She preferred to be outdoors with her father, learning how to best take care of White Willow and its livestock, but she resigned herself to the inevitable and marched up the stairs to the house.

Life was different here in the west and she resigned herself to the fact that it was time she learned how to do the expected women's work.

Someday, White Willow would be hers. She'd spent the last year watching and shadowing her father in his tasks and responsibilities—not that any of the hired hands would ever take direction from a woman. Still, she wanted to know everything she could about running the ranch and figured knowing how to feed them would be one more way for her to contribute.

As Kate tried to focus on the correct measurements of flour, salt, and baking powder, she couldn't help but to glance out the window to watch her father work.

"Child, those biscuits aren't going to make themselves." Fannie pointed at the large bowl with her nose, her hands already immersed in her own basin of sticky dough.

Although Kate was hardly a child at twenty-three, she recognized the importance for a woman in the Wyoming Territory to understand the basics of obtaining a culinary education—especially if she ever hoped to gain a husband—so she turned away from the window, determined to make another hearty attempt.

She cut the butter into small cubes just as Fannie had instructed, then dumped them on top of the flour in her bowl. With a sigh, she shoved her hands into the cool powder to mix it together. The soft feel of it as it sifted through her fingers was cathartic for her restless mind. She pinched the butter, until the pieces were no larger than a pea, then reached for the cup she'd used to mix the white vinegar in with the milk and poured it over the dry blend.

"This is what wooden spoons were made for," she said with an over-exaggerated frown.

"You'll be here all evening, Miss Kate, if you don't just get right in there and knead it all together."

Kate looked down at her bowl, waited a moment, then shoved her hands into the goop and in minutes had it stuck together in a clumpy mess.

"Perfect," Fannie said upon inspection.

"Really?" Kate looked down at her bowl again, wondering if she and the cook were looking at the same dough.

When she'd filled an entire pan and had successfully placed it in the stove, she stood back, wiped her hands on her apron, and nodded in satisfaction.

CRACK!

Dread tore through Kate's chest like a dagger as her head jerked back toward the window.

Da!

She clutched the hem of her dress and lifted as she flung open the door and dashed outside.

Breathe, she reminded herself. *Maybe he just had to put down a sick calf or scare off a coyote.* But even as the thought passed, she knew it was more than that. Something was terribly wrong. She rushed toward the barn.

CRACK!

Another gunshot sounded a little farther away this time, and Kate looked up to see Dell, the dark foreman, firing into the distance. Relief washed over her and she slowed her pace to a stop, hunched over, her hands on her knees, and gasped for air.

Those blasted coyotes were getting bolder as they gradually encroached in on the homestead. Her heart pounded fiercely in her chest and her legs wobbled beneath her. As she pulled herself up into a standing position, a splash of color caught her eye from behind the barn.

She moved slowly at first, making her way around the edge of the building, then she recognized the material of her father's shirt.

"Da?" she called as she picked up her step, newfound trepidation suffocating her insides.

He groaned.

He's alive.

She hurled herself on the ground next to him, tears streaming down her cheeks. She ripped the apron from her body and shoved the material in a wad against the onslaught of blood exuding from the gaping hole in his chest.

"Da…" her voice cracked. She sucked in a breath. "Fannie!" she screamed for the woman who'd followed her outside. "Go get Dell. We need him to go collect the doctor."

"Katie?" her father whispered.

She looked down at him, wiping away the tears with the back of one of her bloodied hands. "What happened, Da?" she used the familiar Irish name. "Was it him?"

Her father opened his eyes, a lone tear escaping the corner as he looked up at her.

"I...I love..." he coughed, "you...my little Katie darlin'." Blood seeped out from between his lips and dripped down the side of his chin. "I'm sorry...It's up to you now." He reached a hand toward her face. Kate held it against her cheek as he closed his eyes. His body relaxed, his hand falling limp in hers.

"No!" she sobbed as she laid her head against his now still body. "Don't leave me, Da."

"Miss Callahan?" Dell placed a hand on her shoulder. "You should go back up to the house. You'll be safer there."

"No!" she screamed through her sobs, shrugging his hand off of her. She needed to still be close to him, to the only family she had left.

She wouldn't leave him.

Not yet.

She wasn't sure how long she'd lain there before the foreman spoke again, the warmth and weight of his hand returning to her shoulder.

"I'll take care of him, Kate."

A well of grief exploded inside of her as she shot a look at him. "Where were you? How could you have let this happen?"

Dell's eyes opened wide, the whites a stark contrast against his face. He shook his head and opened his mouth, but no words came out before he shut it again.

She knew it was unfair of her to place this on him, but right now, she needed someone to blame.

Deputy Marshal Steve Long. The name infringed on her tongue like scum on a pond. *He* was to blame. Thirteen ranchers had now lost their lives to his arrogant and hot-headed delusions. Maybe more.

Kate's jaw flexed, teeth clenched, and her eyes narrowed at the dirt just in front of the opened barn door. It was high time Long paid for his crimes and she would do everything in her power to make that happen.

CHAPTER TWO

Oregon

Noah Deardon pulled the hat from his head as he set a handful of wildflowers he'd clumsily tied with a ribbon down at the base of the stone marker where Persephone's body had been laid to rest. He stood back and smiled his hello. Today made five years since his sickly bride had been consumed with the fever and had passed into her unearthly rest.

They'd only been married three short days, but he'd known the woman nearly his whole life. Persephone Whittaker had been one of his best friends, and while he'd never felt more than friendship for her, he hadn't been able to say no when she'd pleaded with him to not let her die a spinster.

He hung his head.

"You'd like this place, Seph." He looked up and out over the countryside with its wide river and abundant trees surrounding the meadow where they'd played as children, and watched as the swirling clouds took on darkening hues of purple and grey.

A crack of lightning split the sky. Apollo whinnied and

pranced in place.

Noah returned his hat to his head and with one last nod at the grave, sprinted over to his growingly anxious mount.

"I know, boy. We're leaving."

He made it back to the ranch just as the storm cloud sitting above the homestead broke and fat pellets of rain began to fall. He hurried to the barn and dismounted, heaved open the doors, and led Apollo inside. Though it was still early evening, the sky had grown dark and menacing.

Noah heaved the saddle from his horse's back and hung the tack on its appropriate nail. Normally, the methodic pounding of the rain against the barn roof offered soothing relief from his troubles. But tonight, a feeling of unease grew in the pit of his belly. As he brushed Apollo's beautiful black mane, he chuckled to himself at how far his family had come in the last ten years. After their eldest brother, Henry, died unexpectedly after being thrown from the wild stallion he'd been attempting to break, they'd nearly lost everything. But now, things were different.

Their once struggling horse ranch had transformed into one of the most successful cattle ranches in the Northwest. His smile slowly faded as he reached into the bushel at the far edge of the work table and pulled out an apple, holding it out for the horse.

When Apollo greedily lapped it up, Noah laughed out loud, then reached into the bushel to retrieve one for himself. After a few attempts at finding one that wasn't covered in bruises, he tossed it up into the air, caught it, and stepped out into the growing cold. He shoved the doors shut, water streaming from the brim of his hat, and strode toward the house.

He paused as he looked up into the warm scene framed neatly by the square kitchen window. His brother, sister-in-law, and their four little ones gathered around the dinner table, aglow with the flickering lights of several lanterns they had fashioned as a chandelier that dangled from the ceiling.

Jonah, his older brother and benefactor of the ranch, stood just below the lights with a grin spread wide across his face as he pulled his wife into his arms and kissed her smack on the mouth. The children's giggles seeped through the walls of the house and a smile returned to Noah's face.

It's time.

He dipped his head in confirmation.

What he would do next with his life escaped him, but change hung thick in the air. He'd already been at the ranch too long—even though there was no question he would always be welcome. He itched for something more. Something...someone he could call his own.

Noah shook his head and with a whistle on his lips started up the front porch stairs, no idea how he would break the news to his brother and the rest of the family. Whistling seemed to help him sort things out.

Clank.

He froze. His eyes darted back to the kitchen window where he could still see Jonah and his young family busily working on setting the table for supper. Gabe, his father, wasn't due back from Montana for another month, so who would have need of the smaller carriage? There were only a couple of stalls in there, generally used by Jonah's and Emma's mounts. He glanced at the bunkhouse where all the hands would be holed up for the night. Several of them had been talking about a game of cards when he'd left for the meadow, but nothing stirred or appeared out of place.

It was just the horses, he dismissed his concern and turned back for the house.

Clank.

There was no mistaking it this time. Someone lurked in the carriage stable across the yard. He eyed the outbuilding that sat just a few yards from the house as he held his breath in an attempt to listen more closely. The low murmur of a man's voice carried indistinctly on the evening's light breeze, barely audible through the clatter of raindrops striking various surfaces around the yard.

Rustlers had been running rampant in the last few months and getting bolder with their attacks. By the sound of it, there was just one person moving around in there, but if he was wrong, the consequences could be disastrous. If he could get a jump on the thief, he'd be able to handle the situation without incident. He knew he should go get Jonah, but by the time they returned, the miscreant could be gone with at least a pony or two.

One of the horses whinnied from inside the stable and Noah reached for the pistol at his hip.

No gun.

Blast!

Noah padded across the yard, through the rain and puddles, toward the noise. He gingerly wrapped his fingers around the wooden handle of a shovel leaning against the outside wall of the stable. Grateful it hadn't been put away, he stepped toward the open door and waited, his shoulder nudged up against the frame and his back all but touching the wood.

Footsteps crunched against the gravelly dirt.

Noah raised the shovel in the air. When a dark figure appeared in the doorway, he swung, but the culprit ducked before the large spade tool found its mark.

Clang!

The metal blade glanced off of the iron strips that secured the door. Before he could recover, the man had grabbed a hold of the handle and pulled hard, throwing an unrelenting Noah in a circle, sending him spinning through the mud as he stumbled, refusing to release his grip on the spade.

Once he'd regained his footing, Noah wrapped both hands around the wooden stick and yanked back on the tool. He hadn't expected it to be relinquished so easily and the overabundant force of his pull caused it to slip from his grasp and land near the base of the porch steps.

"Blast it all!" he cursed the sliver now embedded in his palm. He shook off the momentary discomfort, his eyes affixed on his opponent.

The intruder had fallen onto one knee, likely thrown off balance by Noah's unexpected pull. Growling, Noah tackled him from behind, slamming him face down into the mud, sending his hat flying.

"Noah!" the man yelled, lifting his head, his voice familiar. "It's me."

The hat that had been stripped off the man's head caught Noah's attention as it dangled from the tip of one of Emma's new spruce saplings. He recognized the big, black Stetson immediately. In the next moment, Noah found himself lying on his back, staring up at an unexpected face.

"Levi? What in tarnation are you doing lurking about in the stable? Come to think of it, what are you doing in Oregon?"

Grunting, his cousin pushed away from him, got to his feet, and offered his hand. Noah reached up to take it, struggling to stand upright. Halfway up, his foot slipped out from beneath him, knocking into Levi's legs, and while they both scrambled to catch their footholds, they ended up falling backward into the mud.

After a brief moment, Levi guffawed loudly and Noah couldn't help but join in the laughter. A light appeared at the top of the porch steps and Jonah stepped out onto the veranda with little Auggie in tow.

"Noah? Is that you?"

"Yes," he called, nearly choking on his water-drenched amusement. He sputtered at the wet clumps of mud that had splashed around his mouth.

"And me," Levi said with a breathy chuckle as he sat up.

"Who's 'Me?'" Jonah asked.

"Me, Levi."

One look at his cousin, mud splattered all over his face and his clothes doused in thick layers of the grimy earth, and Noah starting laughing again. He crawled up onto his knees, then climbed to his feet, then extended his hand to Levi, who chuckled, gladly accepting the help.

Jonah shook his head and turned back into the house.

The soaked and muddy men both glanced at each other and laughed even harder.

"Come on," Noah said as he slung his arm over Levi's shoulders. His cousin mimicked the action, so their arms were woven behind their heads.

"Oh, wait." Levi leaned down, slipping their knot as he reached down to retrieve his hat from the branch of the little tree, then tightened up again.

Together, they stomped up the stairs only to be greeted by Emma, whose arms were folded across her chest, one eyebrow raised—though it was easy to see her struggle to maintain her stern expression or allow the smile that threatened to break through.

The two men dropped their arms to their sides and Noah quickly wiped the grin from his face, opened his eyes wide, and grimaced along with his apology for the filthy state of their clothes. One glance at Levi and he saw that his cousin had done the same.

After a few moments, the smile won and she stepped sideways with a sweep of her hand.

"Levi, did you get your horse all taken care of?" she asked kindly.

He nodded.

"You can barely call that thing a horse. I'm surprised you made it this far with that mule." Jonah laughed.

"Never mind him, Levi. I've put your things in the bedroom behind the kitchen."

"Thank you, Emma."

"Wait," Noah stopped at the threshold, "you knew he was

coming and didn't tell me?"

Emma raised a hand with the smile of hers that said she was up to something. "Talk to your brother about this one."

Jonah, what have you done now?

"Levi?" he called after his cousin who was already halfway to the wash room.

"I'll bring around some fresh towels."

"Uncle Noah. Uncle Noah. You're back," the young twins, Maxwell and Gilbert, ran to the doorway, followed closely by their little brother, Owen, but one look from their mother quelled their enthusiasm.

"Not until he's all cleaned up," she said with an amused shake of her head.

Each of the boys looked appropriately dejected. Noah shrugged his shoulders. Then, he held up a finger as if remembering something. He reached into his back pocket and retrieved a small cloth-wrapped package. The boys' eyes grew wider as he crouched down and pulled back each flap of cloth one at a time. He was grateful that the treats he'd purchased in town hadn't been smashed to bits in his tousle with Levi. When the last fold revealed several small sticks of hard candy and a few lollipops, the children squealed with delight. It turned out that only a few of them had cracked.

"Noah Deardon," Emma scolded, not quite able to conceal the smile that tempted her lips. "You'll spoil their supper."

He stood up, thrusting them behind his back and the children all turned to their mother with eyes exaggeratedly wide, their heads tilted, and tiny hands clasped in front of them.

Emma looked down at them, shaking her head, but alas, they were graced with another of her smiles as she sighed in defeat. "Oh, all right. Just this once."

"Yeah!" they all yelled in unison.

Noah pulled the treats back out from behind him and fanned them out for the children to see.

"You're incorrigible." Emma giggled. Once the boys had their chosen treat, she turned back into the house, shepherding the children indoors. She stood at the door and looked back at Noah meaningfully. "Well, get on with ya, then" she said as she swatted at Noah's shoulder, then instantly pulled her hand away, rubbing her fingers together and exhaling sharply with her nose upturned. "There's extra soap in the cupboard under the window," she called after him.

Noah laughed.

By the time supper was ready and on the table, Noah and Levi had both managed to scrape the mud from their faces, rinse it from their hair, and don clean clothes.

The savory scent of newly cooked meat wafted through the air.

Steak. Noah's mouth watered at the thought. *Bacon.*

He hadn't eaten since breakfast and his stomach protested loudly.

"Now, where is that baby?" Noah asked, ready to hold the newest addition to the Deardon family—at least the newest for now.

Lucy, his baby brother Lucas's wife was due to have her new baby at the end of the next month. Noah loved the smell of clean babies and knew that Emma had just given Auggie a bath. He made a mental note that he should make the trip to Montana next month just to hold Lucas's baby.

Jonah stepped up from behind him and placed Auggie into his arms.

Noah's lips stretched into a grin he was sure consumed his entire face.

Max and Gil stole a questioning glance at their mother. She nodded with a closed lip smile, but did not get up from the table. Their eyes brightened immediately. Noah crouched down, the babe still wrapped in one arm, and he opened the other to the young boys who immediately moved to tackle him around the neck with all their enthusiasm, knocking him

backward enough he had to catch himself from falling. Little
Owen, the three-year-old, hopped down from the table and
joined in with his adorable giggle and short little arms.

"Boys," Emma called after a minute, "that's enough. It's
time to settle down for supper," she announced, standing and
reaching out for her youngest son.

The two oldest climbed up into their chairs, but Owen
stood up straight, unmoving from his spot, and tilted his head
way back to look at Levi. After a moment, he tugged on the leg
of the man's trousers.

Levi dropped onto his haunches with a smile. "What is it,
little man?"

"Is it true you came to take Uncle Noah to find a wife?"

Levi's smile fell and he looked up, 'guilty as charged'
written all over his face.

Noah looked from Emma to Jonah, who both avoided his
gaze, and back at Levi.

A wife?

"A wife?" he repeated, this time aloud.

Levi scooped up the boy and laughed loudly. "Well, I
actually came to see if he was interested in taking over a ranch
of his own."

That piqued Noah's interest and he raised a brow.

"And, it might…" Levi paused, "…come with a wife," he
added with a sheepish, but toothy grin.

Noah's jaw dropped.

"Let's all sit down," Emma suggested. "We can discuss
this while we eat."

He was well aware that his sister-in-law knew he wouldn't
be able to turn down her cooking and, as luck would have it,
she'd made his favorite…steak, fresh-picked corn, and buttery
biscuits. Noah salivated as swirls of steam rose from the large
pot of her delicious bacon-infused beans and drifted beneath
his nose. She must have thought he'd be more keen to go
along with whatever scheme she and his brother had cooked

up with a full belly.

She was probably right.

As hungry as he was, he wasn't sure he wanted to hear what Levi had to say—especially if it involved another marriage for convenience's sake. He turned to walk away.

"I have blackberry custards," Emma tempted.

He stopped.

"With cream," she added.

She'd gotten him. His weakness.

Reluctantly, he slid into a chair at the far side of the table nearest the door. Emma sat down next to him, a satisfied grin on her face.

"So, Levi," Noah asked as soon as grace had been said, "what's this about a ranch?" He might as well get it out in the open rather than skirt around it through an uncomfortable supper.

His cousin set down the biscuit he'd already raised nearly to his mouth. "It's one of the largest in Laramie."

"Wyoming Territory?"

Levi nodded.

He proceeded to recount the misfortune of how the ranch owner had gotten himself shot, leaving his only daughter to run their prospective fortune.

"And this marshal is just going to get away with killing a man in cold blood?" Noah asked incredulously.

"Not if Kate has anything to say about it—though there's not enough proof to have the man arrested," Levi said with an appreciative chuckle. "She's one of the most determined females I have ever met."

"What do you know about the man?" Jonah asked, now leaning forward in his chair.

"More than I want to," Levi responded emphatically. "He's been causing havoc in that town since before the railroad arrived there." Levi leaned against the table. "Eight men, brawling in the street, had the nerve to disregard his warning to stop and five of them were shot dead as a repercussion."

"Is he a gunslinger?" Max asked, his eyes wide and focused on Levi.

"What happened to the other three?" Gil followed quickly with his question. "Did he chase 'em down and kill them too?"

The twins both sat on the edges of their seats, leaning against the table like their father.

Emma shot a horrified look at her children, then at Levi.

"'Fraid not. Only one of those men still lives in Laramie though. The others upped and left with their families. Hey, did you know that I'm a twin too," Levi said as if letting them in on some special secret.

"Really?" Both of the boys' eyes grew wide and their grins spread across their faces.

"Where's your brother?"

Before Levi could answer them, Emma placed her hand on Levi's arm, concern etched on her features. Then she turned to look at Jonah. "Maybe this wasn't such a good idea."

"I'll tell you after supper," Levi whispered to the children.

"My brother can hold his own, my love" Jonah said, confidently. "He might be able to help bring justice to that little town."

Noah shook his head as he swallowed a bite of his food. "Sounds like that ranch, what did you call it, comes at quite a steep price."

"White Willow. One of the neighbors has been working on forming a Vigilance Committee to rid the area of all its lawlessness. It's only a matter of time before the deputy marshal's caught."

"But, like you said before Noah, at what cost?" Emma asked.

"Are they sure it was this Long fella?" Noah asked. He needed more information.

"The Callahan's foreman took a shot at whomever it was

riding away, but the culprit was too far off to identify."

"And now," Noah wanted to clarify, "this Kathryn Callahan has taken out an advertisement for a husband? Like one of those mail-order-bride fiascos, only it's a mail-order-husband?"

"Something like that," Levi said with a chuckle. "But don't ever call her Kathryn," he warned. "She doesn't like that."

Noah bit into his steaming biscuit, pondering the information Levi had just provided, and was momentarily distracted by the rich taste of butter melted over the hot, flakey morsel. He closed his eyes with enjoyment.

"Her ad simply asks for a hardworking man who knows how to run a cattle ranch, is young and able-bodied, someone who is kind and will be faithful. I would tell you to start a correspondence with her, but I'm afraid she won't wait. I know this woman, Noah. If she's looking for a husband, she'll get one. With the Deardon name, combined with the Callahan stead, you'd be a fool to say no. Besides, she's something to look at and very smart. I had a mind to answer her ad myself, but my duties lie elsewhere."

"So, she's all alone right now, trying to protect her land from this Long fellow? It's not a short jaunt from Wyoming to Oregon. What makes you think she's not married yet?"

"You remember my friend, Eamon Walker, the Pinkerton? He's out at her place with a few others keeping watch until I return. And…" he hesitated for a moment, "I may have stopped most of the ads from actually going out."

"You what?" Emma sounded genuinely shocked.

Levi held his hands up in the air. "However, there were two different newspapers I couldn't get to before she'd sent out the information. In my defense, Noah is the right man for this woman, and for the White Willow Ranch," Levi said matter-of-factly. "And I think they are exactly what Noah needs too. It's what you'd call a perfect fit."

A perfect fit? Noah snorted. "When are you heading back to

Wyoming?" he asked, trying to wrap his head around the whole idea.

"First thing tomorrow morning."

Noah swallowed hard. "You don't give a man much time to process, do you?"

Levi, Jonah, and Emma chuckled nervously.

He studied the food on his plate, then glanced over at his four nephews. Wyoming was not just a quick ride into town. If he accepted Levi's offer, the children would likely be grown the next time he saw them and the thought alone made his heart hurt. He popped the last bit of biscuit into his mouth.

It's time.

"You'll have my answer before dawn."

CHAPTER THREE

Laramie, Wyoming, October 28, 1868

"Kate!" The urgency in Dell's voice snapped her eyes open. "Kate! Get up!" The foreman pounded on her bedroom door and she shot out of bed faster than she'd thought possible after the kind of day she'd had.

"What is it?" she asked, trying to restrain the impatience she felt as she threw open the door, one eye still half shut.

He looked at her with surprise.

I must look a sight.

She stood up straight, threw her hand up to her mussed hair, and then felt down her body, relieved she wasn't in her simple nightshift.

She'd been exhausted when she'd retired to her room early and had barely managed to pull off her boots before she'd fallen onto the bed, still dressed in britches and one of her father's old button-down shirts.

"They've done it, Kate! They've finally caught him. Whatever you said to Stella the other day must have worked, because when Long went home with a bullet in his leg, he confessed to her how he'd killed that Hard Luck prospectin' fella in a shootout out at his panning site in the river. After the deputy marshal fell asleep, Stella snuck out to Boswell's place and told him everything she'd learned."

Kate snapped out of her groggy state and grabbed her boots.

"Rollie Harrison is dead?" she asked as she pushed past Dell and hopped toward the front door, attempting to pull on one boot, then the other.

"Yep."

"Well, what are we waiting for? Let's go." She grabbed his arm and pulled him along with her. "I can't believe Nate didn't come get me. He wouldn't have anything on the man if it weren't for me."

She couldn't really be surprised. Nate Boswell, owner of the neighboring ranch and her friend, had been putting together a Vigilance Committee for months and had been extremely vocal about it being no place for a woman. But, rather than accept that, Kate had gone directly to Long's fiancée to plead to her humanity. To her sense of right and wrong. Of justice. It didn't hurt that Stella had been nursing a fat lip when she'd arrived.

Kate opened the front door to find that the Pinkerton Levi had left behind to protect her while he was gone had three horses saddled and ready to ride. Eamon Walker had understood her need for justice and didn't worry about offending her womanly sensibilities like all of the other men in town. She found him refreshing and nodded at him in gratitude.

When she'd first arrived in Wyoming, the idea of riding into town astride a horse at dusk would have scared the life out of her, but she'd ridden enough over the last year or so that it was almost second nature now.

The sun had not completely descended behind the hills, offering enough light for travel as they made their way into town. It didn't take long to reach Laramie from White Willow, as the ranch house sat only a few miles to the east. Commotion surrounded the Frontier Hotel. That had to be where they were taking the brute who'd killed so many people for his greed and pride. Rather than dismount at the livery, Kate rode straight up to the three-story building, dismounted, and left her horse tied to a hitching post out front. As discreetly as she could, she followed the small, hollering, male-dominated crowd around back—Eamon and Dell at her heels.

Kate pushed her way through the mob of men who'd congregated in a clustered mass. Riotous shouts and cheers of vindication and rogue justice rose into the air in waves. When she finally broke through, she stopped short at the gruesome sight that greeted her, but she could not make herself turn away.

Deputy Marshal Long and his half-brothers, the town's lead marshal and the justice of the peace respectively, dangled dead from the rafters of Mr. Olson's unfinished cabin. Kate's legs turned to mush. She dropped down into the dirt and sat there, staring up at the now lifeless man who'd murdered her father.

For some reason, she'd believed that seeing him pay for his crimes would make her feel better, but instead, the hole that had taken residence in her life still sat empty. In that moment, she felt sorry for Stella. The one person in town who would be mourning the deputy marshal's death.

"Kate? You shouldn't be here." Nate strode across the room, a flaming torch in his hand, and reached down to pull her up by the shoulder. "You shouldn't have to see this. I'll take you back to my place and Mary can warm you some milk."

She looked up at him and wriggled her arm from his grasp with indignation.

"How dare you deny me my say, Nathaniel Boswell? You've been a good friend through all of this and I know you were trying to look out for my best interests, but I lost more to that man that you'll ever understand with your wife and daughter at home, safely tucked in their beds." She exhaled heavily and breathed in slowly, calm taking over her hasty reaction. She closed her eyes briefly and quieted her voice. "I deserved to say my piece."

After a short silence, Nate put a hand on her shoulder. "You're right." He paused for an uncomfortable length of time and she looked away from him. "But now, the folks of this town will have some peace," he said. "They'll be able to walk down the streets of town without fear for their lives or that of their loved ones. You, of all people, should understand that." He squeezed her shoulder. "Let me take you home."

"There's no need." Levi Redbourne's low, familiar voice resounded in the air as he stepped out from behind the crowd, a lit torch illuminating his handsome features. Eamon, Dell, and a tall, chisel-jawed stranger stood like intimidating pillars behind him. "I'll take it from here, Boswell."

Emotion welled up inside of her at the sight of the man. She didn't make friends easily, but somehow, Levi Redbourne had become like family to her over the last couple of years. He'd been the brother she'd needed to help her get through the move from Chicago and each of the tragedies they'd experienced since arriving in Laramie.

She could confide in him.

Trust him.

Nate nodded. "Good to see you, Redbourne," he said, extending a hand. "Take care of our girl."

"We intend to," Levi responded, then turned to her, handing the torch to Eamon.

"Levi!" Kate cried, running into his open arms. Tears that she had been holding back since her father's death suddenly found their way down her face.

After a moment, he pushed her shoulders away from him to look down into her face.

"It's done, Katie" he said simply as he slid his arm around her shoulders.

She took a moment to compose herself, breathing, and trying to calm her rapidly beating heart.

"It's done," she echoed in a whisper, tears quickly dissipating and hope returning. She pulled her handkerchief from the back pocket of her britches and wiped her wet face. "Just look at me. I'm a mess." She fiddled with the cloth and self-consciously played with some loose curls at the nape of her neck.

"You're a sight for sore eyes," Levi said as he pulled her back in for a hug. "Let's get you home."

With another deep breath, she concluded she needed to walk away. To look forward and not back. She couldn't change the past, only work hard and have hope for what the future might bring.

A future free from evil men like Deputy Marshal Long.

"Come on," Levi said, keeping one arm around her as he guided her back toward the horses.

As they passed by the stranger who'd come with him, Kate looked up into the most handsome face she'd ever seen. She imagined he looked like one of the Greek gods she'd read about in one of her books. His eyes, aglow with firelight, sent a wave of gooseflesh down her arms and she shot her gaze forward. Surprised by her reaction to him.

No man had ever affected her that way. She'd certainly seen good-looking men before. She was standing right next to one, for heaven's sake, but this was different. There was something about him, in the way he'd looked at her that warmed her from the inside out. She looked over her shoulder to find that he was following them. She'd never seen the likes of him in town before and guessed that he must work with Levi for the railroad.

"I brought you something," Levi said, his lighter tone pulling her from her musings and immediately lifting her spirits.

"Brought it all the way from Oregon. Hand-delivered you might say."

"What *kind* of something?" Kate narrowed her eyes at him, partly because it was hard to make out his features in the waning light, but mostly because she didn't like the mischievous sound in his voice.

Levi Redbourne was always up to something. Though, from some of the stories he'd told her about growing up with his twin brother and all the trouble they'd gotten into back then, she guessed that the war had taken a lot out of him—as it had everyone. But, for those who'd actually witnessed the heart of battle, she imagined it was that much worse. He could be playful without a doubt, but she had a hard time imagining him as a 'hooligan.'

Levi looked back over his shoulder at the stranger and smiled.

"It wouldn't be a surprise if I told you, now would it?" he finally answered. "You'll find out soon enough."

"Should I be scared?"

Levi chuckled. "It's exactly what you asked for."

"That doesn't help." Kate could not think of a single thing for which she'd asked him or anyone else. And nothing she'd expressed interest in would come from Oregon.

They passed by several men whom Nate had recruited for the committee and several more who she guessed had been at the Belle of the West saloon when Long and his brothers had been arrested. Most of them were excitedly mumbling amongst themselves and barely gave notice to her and the others as they walked by. The town seemed to finally be able to breathe with the reprehensible lawmen gone.

When they reached the boardwalk in front of the hotel, a woman leaned quietly against the log-lined walls, her face hidden behind a handkerchief, her shoulders shaking.

Kate stepped out from beneath Levi's arm and walked over to her, reaching out and placing a hand on her arm.

"Stella?"

The woman whipped her head up as if startled, then met Kate's eyes. Dark-colored tears streaked her face and colored her cloth tissue. One of her eyes and her cheek were swollen, the bruising detectable beneath the face painting cosmetics Stella generally wore.

To the devil with that man.

Kate bit back the words, but it irked her to no end when she learned of any man who would lay a heavy hand to the woman he claimed to love or intended to wed. She placed her fingers under Stella's chin and raised it slightly to get a better look at her in the beams from the torchlight.

"He can't hurt you anymore," she spoke in a quiet, coaxing voice, raising a finger to wipe away another tear that had just escaped the corner of the woman's eye.

Without warning, Long's fiancée sprung into Kate's arms and continued to sob, her whole body shaking uncontrollably. Kate stroked her hair, holding the woman while she cried. While she mourned the loss of the man she'd thought to love.

After a few moments, Stella hiccupped as she pulled herself together.

"It was you, Miss Callahan. You gave me the courage to do what was right. I didn't mean to get him hung, but he wasn't a good man, and I had to stop him from killin' any more folks." She looked up at Kate with wide eyes. "I'm so sorry about your pa. If I'd been stronger before…"

"Shhhh…" Kate shook her head. "What happened to my da wasn't your fault. You were very brave going all the way out to Mr. Boswell's ranch and telling him what you knew. Thank you."

Stella nodded.

Hiccup.

She raised her fingers to cover her mouth.

"Do you need anything?" Kate asked out of habit.

Stella shook her head.

"There's nothing left for me here in Laramie. I think I am going to head up to Montana. Reverend Jones just obtained a job with a new parish and Cindy, I mean Mrs. Jones," she corrected, "invited me along. Says there are a lot of good men looking for wives there."

"I hope the best for you, Stella."

"You could come too, you know," she said with a sniff, then looked up as if noticing Levi and the other men with her for the first time. "Or," she leaned a little closer and spoke in whispered tones, "you might just be lucky enough to find a good man right here in town." Her head jerked only once in the affirmative.

Kate opened her mouth, then closed it again. She hadn't told anyone in Laramie about her ad for a husband, but she'd already vetted the unattached men in town and there was certainly no one local she had any intention of marrying.

Levi was more like a brother to her than anything else. Of course, he fit the bill, everything she'd asked for—came from a family of ranchers, kind, and she had no doubt in her mind that he would be unyieldingly faithful to the woman lucky enough to capture his heart.

She glanced over at the man and stared for a long moment. *Nope. Nothing.* There wasn't any kind of spark or feelings, other than brotherly affection, when she looked at him. She shrugged. Besides, Levi worked for the railroad and she needed someone who could plant his roots right here in Laramie and help her run the ranch.

"I'd better get back," Stella said with a sniff. "The pastor is letting me stay in the room at the back of the church tonight. I just can't bring myself to go home. Not now." Stella's solemn face returned as she brushed past Kate, blowing her nose as she bustled toward the small, newly erected chapel—so out of place against the backdrop of several all-night saloons.

As she turned around, Mr. Dixon, the town undertaker scuttled down the boardwalk toward the cabin turned gallows, holding out his lantern, his measuring tape dangling from his pocket.

It's done, she reminded herself again as she joined the others where the horses had been tied. She was pleased to see that her mount and another she didn't recognize had been strapped to a buckboard with lanterns dangling on either side.

She glanced at each of the men now surrounding her, her eyes stopping momentarily on the stranger Levi had brought with him. There were definitely sparks with him. He tipped his hat and smiled, revealing straight, white teeth—a feature hard to come by this far west. Her belly did a little flip-flop inside.

Who is he?

"You fellas had any supper?" she asked, forcing herself to look away from the mysterious man who'd caught her interest. "Fannie made fried potatoes and ham. I'm sure there's still some left in the kitchen."

Emmett Callahan had hired the woman to help Kate learn how to cook. With all of the duties the ranch required of her, Kate had neglected to be a good domestic student. She was grateful, however, that Fannie had agreed to stay on after her father died—something that most of the ranch hands had refused to do. No one wanted to work for a woman out here.

A coyote howled and Kate glanced out into the vast darkness beyond the town. She didn't hear if any of the men had responded to her earlier question as her attention was now focused elsewhere.

Though the moon was full, it sat too low in the sky to provide much light for the ride home. Her heart beat fast and her shoulders tightened. The urgency that had fueled her journey into town had fled, and she had to remind herself that she would be surrounded by able-bodied men. There was nothing to worry about. The ranch wasn't far. It was only the dark. The dark couldn't hurt her.

"Ready?" A low, warm voice asked at her side.

She jumped.

"You startled me." When Kate looked up, she was greeted by Levi's friend with the sultry eyes. She glanced down at his extended hand and bit her bottom lip as she slid hers into its warmth.

He helped her up onto the seat, then turned to say something to Levi, who'd already mounted a horse much too short for his long, muscular legs. It didn't suit him.

Kate gathered the reins and waited.

"Excuse me, ma'am." The gentleman with the white smile and perfect jaw climbed up next to her on the wagon seat and handed her an additional lantern.

He's driving me home?

Her mother would turn over in her grave if she knew that Kate had allowed herself to be unaccompanied in the front seat of a buckboard with a man whose name she didn't even know, let alone letting him drive her home. She held up the lantern to get a better look at his face. Strung on one of his coat buttons dangled a postage delivery tag and she couldn't help but see her name written in big fancy letters.

"May I?" she asked.

The man nodded.

Kate picked up the tag and read,

> *To: Kate Callahan, Laramie*
> *One mail-order-husband—*

Husband? She shot a look at him, then back down at the tag and read it aloud. The speed of her heart increasing with every word.

"Mr. Noah Deardon, first cousin of Levi Redbourne..." She cleared her throat. "Knowledgeable of cattle ranching. Kind to a fault. Young and able-bodied." She paused, heat flooding her face. "And a man who will be faithful on his word—on the word of Levi Redbourne. Hand delivered by Levi Redbourne."

Kate looked up at the man who was shaking his head, but smiling all the same.

"I should probably introduce myself, ma'am." He looked at her with eyes that glinted like steel in the moonlight, sending gooseflesh down her arms. Again. "I am Noah Deardon, first cousin to Levi Redbourne, and all of those other things. I am here in response to your ad—one mail-order husband."

The dark, weighted cloud that had loomed over her for months, lifted and for the first time in a very long while she had hope.

CHAPTER FOUR

Even dressed in men's clothing, Kate Callahan was easily the most beautiful woman Noah had ever laid eyes on. Her unkempt hair and flushed cheeks only added to her appeal.

He shook his head and smiled as the woman seated next to him read the blamed tag Levi had insisted he wear. He felt like a fool, if ever there was one, but if it evoked another smile from the lady, he was happy to oblige.

"You're my package? Hand-delivered from Oregon?" She breathed a laugh.

"Guilty as charged."

"Only Levi would bring me a...a husband."

As they pulled out toward White Willow, Noah stayed close behind Levi and the others, careful not to get separated. The last thing he needed to do was to prove himself the fool by getting lost in the dark.

"What's wrong with you?" Her question startled him.

"Ma'am?"

"There aren't many men who would be willing to give up their lives and move a thousand miles away from home to marry a woman he'd never met. So, what's wrong with you? Why aren't you already married? You're certainly handsome enough. And you look strong and able bodied."

Noah was glad it was dark outside as he could feel the heat rush to his face and neck at her assessment of him. He sat up a little taller and cleared his throat.

"Well," he had to think for a moment.

What *was* wrong with him?

"I don't always take my boots off before walking into the house. I whistle when I have a lot on my mind and sometimes that annoys my brother. I often let my cousins—particularly that one," he said as he pointed at Levi a few yards ahead, "talk me into doing some cockamamie things."

"Like moving across country to marry a woman you've never met?"

"Yes, like that." He laughed.

She laughed too.

Kate was straightforward. No nonsense. It was refreshing. Most of the women he'd courted or been around had a tendency to play coy and often sent mixed signals. He didn't need a woman who played games. He needed someone with a good head on her shoulders, someone willing to stand beside him. Work alongside him. Someone he could take care of. Love.

After everything he'd seen tonight, he hoped that someone might be Miss Kate Callahan. From the moment he'd caught her staring at him, there had been something between them that he couldn't explain, and he wondered if she'd felt it too. It was almost like a spark.

She was beautiful and strong, resilient, yet he'd seen the compassion in her face as she'd spoken to the young woman on the boardwalk. The woman who'd been betrothed to the man who'd taken Kate's father away from her. That alone would have impressed him.

"So, why did you agree to come to Wyoming? It's not the

green forests and hills of Oregon, that's for sure." Her voice brought him out of his reverie and he cleared his throat again.

He'd thought about that question many times over the course of the last month on the trail. He could give her a nice flowery answer. Something he thought she might like to hear, but if he didn't want a woman who played coy, he certainly didn't want to be a man doing the same thing.

He glanced over at her. She smiled, her eyes fixed on his. A light breeze swooped across the landscape, flickering the lantern's flame and catching her hair like a blanket drying on a line.

Kate shivered.

Noah slowed the horses a bit as he reached into the back of the wagon and pulled out a thick woolen blanket.

"Was it that obvious?" She asked as she set the lamp down on the step in front of her and wrapped the covering around her shoulders. When she was settled again, he could feel her eyes on him and she raised the light again. "Wyoming?"

"Honestly, I needed a place of my own. My older brother, Jonah, has taken over the family's ranch back home. He's married with four little ones."

He missed those four little ones more than he cared to admit and it had only been a couple of weeks.

"Lucas is my younger brother. He moved to Montana several years ago to work on our grandfather's ranch. He met his perfect match, Lucy, and they now have two children and are expecting their third this month."

He still regretted that he'd never gotten to know their estranged grandfather before he'd passed away. But a few years back he'd at least been able to make the trip to Whisper Ridge where he'd gotten to know Lucy, his Montana nephews, and a handful of relatives he'd had no idea had even existed.

"So, you've got just the two brothers?" Kate turned in her seat enough that she was almost facing him.

"And Henry," he said, focusing fully on the trail in front of them. "Henry was the oldest."

"Was?"

"He died about ten years ago, while breaking a mustang." He dared a glance in her direction.

Her head bowed.

"My condolences."

"It was a long time ago," he shrugged, though he wished he could say he didn't think about it much anymore. That day still haunted him in his dreams.

Enough about me.

"I was sorry to hear about your father."

"Thank you."

"Levi said he was a good man."

"He was."

She obviously didn't want to talk about it either. They rode for a few minutes in a comfortable silence as the stars came out to play, peeking out between the dramatic strokes of clouds as they transformed in the sky. A soft tune danced around in his mind and he started to whistle.

"That's lovely," she said. "What is it?"

"Ah, I don't know. Sometimes I just get a tune in my head that won't go away.

"I love music."

"I understand that you didn't grow up ranching," Noah said, wanting to hear her voice again. "From Chicago?"

"Why, Mr. Deardon, I think you have me at a disadvantage."

As they passed through a large wooden archway, the homestead came into view. It was dark except for the room at the front of the house where a man's obscured silhouette was visible in the window.

Noah reached down for the rifle he'd holstered at the side of the buckboard. From what he'd learned about Kate and the ranch, the only men that would be in the main house were Dell and Eamon, and both of them were still mounted just ahead of him in front of the house.

Levi'd drawn his pistol. He'd seen the man too.

Loud laughter came from one of the out buildings where a dim light flickered. It had to be the bunkhouse where the last couple of hired hands would be settling in for the night.

Noah didn't want to alarm Kate, so he continued talking.

"What about you? You are beautiful and smart. I'd bet there's any number of men around these parts that would marry you and help run your ranch. Why place an ad?"

"Have you seen the men around here? They are either married, or…well, no thank you." Kate stood, but Noah put a protective arm up in front of her.

"What's wrong?" she asked, sitting back down on the bench.

"Just stay here. We'll be right back."

"I don't think so," she said, pulling a small revolver from the pocket of her britches. "If there's a problem on my ranch, I'm perfectly capable of handling it."

"I have no doubt of that." Noah jumped from the wagon, ran around to the other side, and raised a hand to help Kate down.

As soon as her feet touched the ground, she started for the door, but stopped and waited for them at the bottom of the stairs while they hitched their horses and the wagon to the rail post.

After Levi and Noah took their places on either side of the door, and Eamon and Dell had disappeared around the back, Noah nodded that they were ready for her to barge inside.

She reached for the handle on the door.

Noah took a deep breath, prepared for the worst.

She pushed.

CHAPTER FIVE

"Miss Kate," Fannie rushed forward. "This man says he's come a long way in answer to an advertisement you placed in his local paper. I told him you had gone into town, but he insis—"

"It's all right, Fannie." Kate smiled at the woman, grateful for the lit lamps throughout the room. "Thank you for entertaining our *guest* while I was away."

He couldn't be much of a gentleman if he'd insisted on sitting in a house alone with a woman—even if Fannie was old enough to be his grandmother.

"Clifford Thomas, ma'am," the man said, already on his feet and taking a step toward her. "From Abilene. I apologize for calling at such a late hour, but I just arrived in town and wanted to meet the woman I've come to marry." He flashed a smile that would be hard to forget.

Kate's jaw dropped.

She'd been in Laramie for nearly two years and in that time the only men who'd paid any attention to her were either already spoken for or those who frequented the saloons. Well, except for Dell. Since placing the ad over a month ago, she'd received correspondence from only one man from Montana, but nothing else. Now, two seemingly respectable suitors had appeared in one day. That made three.

"You're an awfully long way away from home, Mr. Thomas. I wasn't aware that my ad would reach Texas."

He wasn't as tall as Noah and he had dark hair, but he also looked as if he knew his way around a ranch.

"Well, actually, ma'am, I just finished a drive up through Colorado and a few of the boys mentioned your advertisement."

Mr. Thomas's eyes unexpectedly grew wide and he glanced from one position over her left shoulder to another position over her right. She smiled a little, realizing that Levi and Noah must be standing directly behind her. She could feel them scrutinizing every inch of this man and could imagine how imposing a backdrop they would be. He looked down at the drawn gun in her hand and swallowed hard.

"Were y'all expectin' someone else?"

Kate hastily tucked the gun into her belt and turned back to look over her shoulder to where Noah stood, eyebrow raised, staring at the man like a skilled wrangler staring down a wild horse.

"Mr. Thomas, I am Kate Callahan and this is Levi Redbourne and Noah Deardon."

Dell and Eamon took that moment to come through the kitchen and into the living area, both with weapons drawn as well.

Mr. Thomas nodded at each of them, his hands raised slightly in front of him. "Are all of you here for Miss Callahan's hand?"

Everyone just continued to stare at the man, until finally Noah stepped forward next to Kate.

"Just me," he said in a rich, deep voice that sent butterflies sprawling through her belly. She could get used to that sound.

Mr. Thomas looked Noah up and down as she was sure

Noah had already done to him.

"You don't mind a little friendly competition now, do ya, friend?" Mr. Thomas asked.

"Not when it's someone worth competing for." Noah looked down and winked at her. Warmth spread over her whole body.

Compete? For me? She wasn't sure she liked the sound of that.

"Where are you staying, Mr. Thomas?"

"Well, ma'am, as I said before, I just got into town and I thought I'd be staying here. At the ranch. With my wife. Didn't make no other arrangements."

Eamon coughed behind his hand, which Kate suspected hid a chuckle.

"Surely, Mr. Thomas, you didn't think we'd just march down to the chapel and have Reverend Jones marry us? How could you think I would make you a part of my life on this ranch without so much as having a conversation?"

He cleared his throat. "From your ad, I figured you'd want to get started as soon as possible. It sounded like you needed a bit of help getting this place in order. I thought we'd spend a few hours talking, sure, but it's not like you're looking to be courted? You put an ad in a newspaper for a husband, not for a suitor or business partner."

Kate could not believe her ears. He was a blamed fool if he didn't think a woman needed to be courted—by her suitor or husband, it didn't matter. She hadn't been looking for love exactly. She'd learned from her parents that love grew over time, but respect and consideration were not negotiable.

"We've not exchanged any correspondence nor do I know anything about you. We haven't been acquainted for all of five minutes and, frankly, I find your arrogance off-putting."

Be polite, Kate.

Maybe placing that ad had been a mistake.

She looked up at Noah, with his broad shoulders, tousled

blond hair, and easy smile.

Maybe not.

"I'm sorry, Mr. Thomas, I know you've come a long way. There is a lot of work to be done. My father purchased a herd of three-hundred head just before he died. They have been delayed in Denver, but I am assured they will be delivered in the next couple of weeks. Until then, I have time to decide what, or who as the case may be, is best for me. And my ranch."

"I understand completely, Kate. May I call you Kate?" He didn't wait for an answer. "Would you mind terribly if I stayed in the bunkhouse until you've reached your decision?"

"Do you know anything about the cattle business, Thomas?" Levi asked incredulously before she could respond. "Are you a kind person? Loyal? No one here knows the answers to any of those questions. You don't just expect her to take *your* word for it?"

It was obvious he'd taken a dislike to the man.

"Well, yeah." Mr. Thomas nodded. "I'm sorry, who are you exactly?"

"Do you have any credentials? Anyone who can vouch for you?"

"In Abilene, of course." His jaw clenched momentarily before continuing. "Or the trail boss from the drive to Colorado would—"

"Fannie?" Kate interrupted. The last thing she needed after the day she'd had was to have a full out brawl in her living room. It had been a long day and her body just wanted to crawl back into her bed and sleep for a few days. Unfortunately, running a ranch did not allow for such luxuries.

She looked over at the older woman who'd been observing the entire interaction from the doorway into the kitchen. "Do you have any of that ham or those fried potatoes left from supper?"

Fannie's eyes grew wide. "I saved what was remaining,

Miss Kate, but not enough to feed five grown men. I'm afraid what's there is a might cold." She turned around and headed back into the kitchen. "I suppose I could warm some of yesterday's stew to go along with it."

"Would you mind terribly, Fannie?" Kate called after her. "I think these gentlemen all need a little food in their bellies," she said this last part more to herself than the cook. She needed the distraction.

CHAPTER SIX

Noah's stomach grumbled with a month's lack of good hearty meals of meat and potatoes, but the food could wait. There was something about this Clifford Thomas that made him want to punch the man in the nose and send him right back to Abilene with all of his presumptions and lack of respect. He watched the man jaw at his food like he was a prince in his palace and lost his appetite.

He needed air.

He and Levi had been on the road for most of the day. Then, when they'd arrived in town, he'd witnessed a full on lynching of the man Levi had told him about—the one who had killed Kate's father. To top it all off, he met the woman he'd travelled all this way to marry, only to discover he wasn't her only would-be suitor. He was exhausted and looked forward to a good night's sleep in a real bed. His head would be clearer in the morning.

He stood.

"Well, thank you kindly for the supper, Miss Fannie, and for the pleasure of making your acquaintance, Miss Callahan. I best be heading out if I'm going to make it back to town in time to get any sleep tonight." Luckily, the ranch was only a few miles out of town. He should be able to make it to the inn he'd seen at the far edge within the hour.

Kate stood as well.

"I hope it wasn't presumptuous of me, Mr. Deardon, but I already had Dell put both Levi's and your things in the bunkhouse." She stood, her plate in hand, and walked over to the sink to deposit her dishes, then turned back to look at him.

"That's mighty kind of you, ma'am." He reached up and tipped the air where the brim of his hat normally rested on his head. "I'd be much obliged. Thank you."

"Are you sure you wouldn't like something to eat?" she asked, pointing at the large pot of stew warming on the stove.

"I'm real grateful for your hospitality, ma'am. The horses have been out there tied to the post a might too long. Apollo needs to be attended to—brushed down and fed."

"I'll show him to the stables, Kate," Levi said, joining Noah at the door.

"I think I'll turn in after that, if it's all right with you, of course," Noah said, pulling the door open. "It's been a long day."

She nodded. "Of course."

He managed a smile before he took a step over the threshold, then stopped, leaning back through the door to look at her. "Miss Callahan, it's been a real pleasure to meet and talk with you. Thank you."

He walked out into the yard and over to the hitching post where Levi's mule of a horse was tied up next to Apollo and the chestnut mount Kate had ridden into town.

"You really need to get a new horse," Noah told his cousin with amusement. "When you're not riding the train, you need a mount that will get you out to some of these towns without worrying your pony is going to up and die on you."

"Mock all you want, but this little fella got me all the way to Oregon to collect you, now didn't he? And back."

"That he did. Just don't say I didn't warn you."

"I know," Levi relented. "If my brothers saw what I was riding, I'd never hear the end of it. Especially from Cole. He's been working with a new stallion, imported from overseas and bought at auction. Mama says he's even riding bareback."

Noah took Apollo and Kate's chestnut horse by the reins, the wagon still attached, and followed Levi toward the barn. After backing the buckboard into the corner, next to what looked like a winter sleigh, he unhitched the team, then he and Levi led all three mounts to the stable where they discovered a couple of stalls had already been cleaned and swept out for them.

"Here, I'll take her." One of the ranch hands appeared behind them, reaching out for the reins on Kate's mare. "It's nice to see you again, Mr. Redbourne," he said with a nod, then turned to Noah. "Name's Virg."

Noah handed him the requested reins.

"Noah."

"Mr. Walker told me you might be staying a while. Let me know if you need anything." He tipped his hat and headed to another stall to take care of the mare.

"Thank you," Noah called after him.

A large stack of fresh straw mounded in one of the empty stalls. He grabbed a pitchfork off the wall and took several large measures of the bedding, tossing it into Apollo's stall.

Silence passed between the men for a number of minutes before Noah started to whistle. The ranch and its owner were a lot to take in. After a few more minutes, Levi finally peeked over the stall, his arms perched on the short partition separating them, his chin resting on his hands.

"So, what do you think of Miss Kate Callahan?" he asked.

Noah had noted a barrel of oats and a scoop in the corner next to the work table and stepped over to retrieve them. How could he tell his cousin that Kate was already more than he'd ever dreamed she would be, that not only was she the most beautiful woman he'd ever had the pleasure of meeting, but he'd thoroughly enjoyed her company? He wasn't worried as much about Mr. Thomas and the man's ill manners as he was about the others that would surely start arriving. He couldn't allow himself to fall for a woman who may never be his. He'd married for the wrong reasons the first time, and the next time would be the last time. It had to be right.

"I can see why you were tempted to settle down," he said coolly as he lifted the saddle from Apollo's back and hung it over the partition next to Levi. "She's pretty and no nonsense. I like that." He unhooked the brush that hung just outside of the stall and proceeded to groom the gelding's sleek grey coat and long black mane. "How many men do you think will answer her ad?"

"I don't know. Maybe a dozen or so. It only got through to two different newspapers. One in Colorado and the other in Montana. Why?"

"I just need to know what I'm up against and how quickly I need to win her over."

"You like her. Don't you?"

Noah could not stop the smile that cracked through. "It's too early to tell, but if I am going to have a fighting chance, I need to get to know her better. And the ranch. I'll ride out first thing tomorrow and get a good look at the herds, the pastures, and the outbuildings."

Usually, a ranch this size would have at least a dozen hands, but the foreman, Dell, had told him that only three had agreed to stay on after Mr. Callahan died—Virg, Oscar, and Cal, if he remembered correctly.

"I'd like to speak with Dell and make note of any repairs that need to be made. Also, I heard the clerk at the telegraph office mention that there are several thousands of acres for sale out this way and I would like to look at buying some."

"Whoa, slow down there, Noah. You're going to hurt yourself with all that planning." Levi moved out in front of the tack room and leaned back against one of the beams, his ankles crossed, and his arms folded.

Noah laughed. "It's not worth doing if you don't do it right." He stepped out of the stall and latched it shut, placing the pitchfork back on its proper hook. "Granddad was very generous with our inheritance and I want to put it to good use."

"I wouldn't know about that…yet," Levi said, shaking his head. "I'm not too worried about it, though. If it doesn't happen in time and I don't get the money, would it really be that bad? It's not as if my family struggles. Financially, I mean."

"It's not a trivial amount, Levi. You could do a lot of good with the money Granddad left you. However, you are still quite a ways off from the 'end of your twenty-fifth year.' You'll be fine."

Liam Deardon had believed that unmarried men over the age of twenty-five were a menace to society. Thus, he had been very specific in his will that each portion of his grandchildren's inheritance was dependent upon them getting married before their twenty-sixth birthday.

Noah hadn't felt deserving of the sizeable sum he'd received after he'd wed Persephone Whittaker and had been very reluctant to spend any of it until he was good and married to a woman he loved. If that woman was Kate, all the better.

"Not that far off? I'm twenty-three."

The horse in the next stall nickered quietly and stuck his head out over the short gate wall to say hello.

Noah laughed and reached into his saddle bag for another apple. He'd spotted a whole bushel at the livery in town and had purchased some of them from the liveryman when he'd rented the buckboard this evening.

"Yes, you're a right old man." He held up the lantern and

placed the apple on his open palm. When the light-colored steed had finished eating the treat, Noah rubbed the mount's neck and face. "What a beautiful horse. I've never seen one like him."

"And you probably won't. Around here anyway," Levi said as he came closer.

"What do you mean?"

"Well, not that I've seen one as well-mannered as this," he reached up and scratched behind the horse's jaw, "but if you ask me, that's an Arabian."

"How do you know?"

"You remember when I told you about my kid brother, Cole's, new horse. Well, he saw one of these at auction just before I left for Oregon. It was just a colt, but Cole fell in love. He was a sleek, black color. Although, this one is lighter, he has the same characteristics as Cole's. He looks like a cross between a Quarter Horse and a mustang. See here," Levi pointed to the bulge on the horse's forehead. "He's an Arabian all right."

"Is he one of Kate's?" Noah had worked with a lot of horses—mustangs mostly, but this one seemed special somehow.

"I've never seen him before. It's more likely, he belongs to Thomas."

"What's a drover on a cattle run doing with a horse like that?" Noah asked, wheels turning wildly in his head.

"I don't know, but it can't be something good."

Noah'd had a bad feeling about the man from the start. Now, that warning was amplified tenfold.

"Shhhh." Levi placed a finger over his mouth as he pushed himself away from the beam in front of the tack room and leaned up against the front door, peering out into the dark.

Voices carried into the stable from the yard. Noah immediately recognized the Irish lilt of Kate's speech. He peeked around the opposite side of the stable door to see Dell,

Mr. Thomas, and Miss Callahan walking toward the bunkhouse.

He forced the sharp pang in his belly away as he pulled back out of sight—not that they would be able to see him in this light anyway.

"You *do* like her," Levi taunted.

"Did you suspect it would be any different?" Noah shook his head. "Aren't you the one who brought me all the way out here because you knew she was the kind of woman any man in his right mind would want?"

"Of course, I knew. I'm just glad to hear you're in your right mind." Levi chuckled.

Now that the horses had been taken care of, Noah was ready to turn in for the night. He had already made a mental list of things he needed to do in the morning—return the buckboard he'd rented from the livery, ride the perimeter of the property, and observe the current workings of the ranch. If he was going to make a difference here, he needed to know what he was up against. Of course, he wouldn't be good for anything tomorrow if he didn't get a decent night's sleep.

"Goodnight, Kate. Mr. Thomas." The foreman's distant voice faded as he headed for the bunkhouse.

Noah stuck his ear to the door. He didn't want to eavesdrop, but his gut told him not to leave this Thomas fella alone in the dark with Kate. He took a deep breath, debating whether or not he should wait for them to finish their conversation, but decided better of it. He stepped out into the yard and strode toward the bunkhouse, Levi at his heels.

"Why, Mr. Deardon." Kate looked up at him as if she were surprised to see him. "Is everything all right?" The moonlight spilled down the side of her face, adding a child-like quality to her features. She was even more beautiful than he'd remembered.

It took a moment before he realized he hadn't responded. He cleared his throat, heat collecting under his collar.

"Fine," he responded, cursing the crack in his voice.

"Horses are all situated for the night and we're just about to turn in. Thought we'd take Mr. Thomas along with us."

"But, I was saying goodnight to Miss Callahan," the man protested, but Levi took him by the arm and led him away from Kate.

"Goodnight, Miss Callahan," Noah said on all of their behalf as he reached up and tapped his imaginary hat once again.

"Goodnight," she whispered, turning back for the house.

Noah watched as she ascended the stairs and he sucked in a breath when she turned back to look at him over her shoulder, her long, wavy mane blowing lightly in the cool autumn breeze. She reached up and tucked a lock behind her ear and Noah groaned.

It was going to be a long night. He had a lot to think about.

She turned back for the stairs.

Crash!

Her hand had slipped, missing the handrail completely, her body colliding hard into the feeble barrier. The wood gave way, sending Kate tumbling off the four-foot drop to the ground with a squeal.

Noah was at her side in an instant.

"Miss Callahan?" he called, alarmed when she didn't respond. "Kate?" he tried again, all too aware he'd used her given name.

A soft moan escaped her lips and he closed his eyes in gratitude that she hadn't gotten herself killed.

"I'm all right," she finally said with a groggy tone as she attempted to sit up on her own.

Noah placed a hand in the small of her back to keep her from falling backward, her proximity wreaking havoc on his senses.

After a moment, she made a move to stand, but quickly sat back down again, amongst the piles of splintered wood.

"Maybe I'll just sit here a moment and lick my wounded pride."

Noah laughed.

She'll be just fine.

"Let's get you inside," he said, holding out his hand to her. "The air is a might chilly tonight."

When her fingers touched his, a light, tingling jolt spread up his arm, but he couldn't pull away. He attempted to help her to her feet, but her ankle buckled beneath her.

"Upsi-daisy," he said, her hand still firm in his grasp.

Kate started to giggle, but winced in pain.

"I think I may have hurt a little more than my pride," she said, rubbing her ankle.

Without waiting any longer, Noah released her hand and reached down, scooping her up easily into his arms. He climbed the porch stairs, opened the door, and carried her inside.

"Where are your quarters?" he asked, unable to keep the obvious rasp from his voice.

She turned toward him, her hand resting at the button of his shirt, her face so close to his he could feel her breath on his lips. He looked down into her wide, trusting eyes.

Big mistake.

He groaned, forcing himself to look away. If being this close to her was going to be a common occurrence, he needed to win her over. Fast.

"Your room?" he asked again. Maybe he should have just left her on the couch for propriety's sake, but somehow it didn't seem right leaving her alone to fend for herself on an injured foot. Especially, after Levi had told him about her debilitating fear of the dark.

"It's just down the hall," she said, a little quiver in her voice.

Careful, Deardon, he warned himself.

He carried her to the bed and set her down at the end,

feeling around on the table, hoping to find a lantern there. He wasn't disappointed. It only took a moment to light the lamp. He crouched down and gently lifted her foot, pushing back the material of her trousers and carefully removing her boots to expose her ankle, already swollen from the fall. Kate bit her lip as he pushed her foot forward and side to side, assessing the extent of the injury. Nothing more than a whimper escaped her lips. He admired her tolerance for pain.

"You need to keep that foot elevated," he said as he gently swung her legs atop the bed and grabbed one of her pillows to place beneath the injured one. "I'll be right back."

He left the lantern in her room and headed into the kitchen. He stumbled across another lamp. The matches sat just at its base, and he lit the wick before looking for some clean rags and the water pump. He found the sink, but there was no pump.

Add that to the list.

He discovered a drawer full of mid-size towels, grabbed a few, and headed out to the wash area he'd spotted several yards from the homestead. A water pail dangled from the handle. Once he started pumping, it didn't take much for the water to begin flowing. He doused two of the three towels under the chilly water and set them in the pail. Back home they had a local vendor who sold ice that could keep the rags cold enough to be useful and wondered if they had such a thing here. Not that it mattered at this hour.

When he returned to Kate's room, her eyes were closed and her breathing heavy and even. She was asleep.

He imagined it had been a long, emotional day for her as well. He couldn't conceive of the heartache she must have endured having her father taken from her in such a brutal way, then to have seen the man who'd killed him hanging from the rafters of that little, unfinished cabin.

Noah thought of how hard it had been when he'd lost his mother.

That was different. It had been her choice to leave and never look back. She'd left many years ago. He didn't know where she lived or even if she was still alive. He shook the thought of her from his mind and focused on wrapping Kate's ankle.

When the cool rag touched her skin, she stirred, but did not wake. He tucked the blankets up around her shoulders and face, so she would not get a chill in the night and smiled when she snuggled more deeply into them. She was so young to have suffered so much. He glanced down at her sleeping peacefully, and, for the first time in a long time, he had knots in his belly. He could see already that Kate alone was worth the fight.

CHAPTER SEVEN

Kate laid in her bed, looking up at the ceiling, fresh morning sunlight spilling into her bedroom like syrup over hotcakes, filling the space around her with a warm cheerfulness. It was brighter than her normal wake time and she realized that she'd overslept. She turned, the pain radiating from her ankle reminding her that she'd fallen through the railing last night right in front of Mr. Deardon and her face flooded with warmth.

She'd made a fool of herself, but had to admit she'd liked being in Noah's arms as he'd carried her into the house.

Shame on you, Katie Callahan.

Maybe it had all been just a dream. She attempted to wiggle and twist her foot.

Ouch. Bad idea. Not a dream.

Her ankle was wrapped in soggy towels that had seeped onto the pillow beneath her leg and she smiled to herself as she thought of her tall, blond rescuer. With a little effort she was able to sit herself up and look out her bedroom window, noticing the light frost creating a vignette around the corners of the glass.

Winter was coming and they still had so much to do to prepare. She gingerly reached down to her foot and removed the wet cloths. The skin looked purplish in color around her ankle and swollen enough that she doubted she'd be able to put much pressure on it, let alone pull a boot over it. Nevertheless, she cautiously swung her legs over the side of the bed and slid down off the mattress in an attempt to stand.

A sharp, stabbing pain shot through her foot.

Definitely not.

The methodic pounding of a hammer against nails broke the blissful silence of the morning.

"Good morning, Miss Kate," Fannie walked in, a tray in hand, filled with biscuits, eggs, bacon, and a cup of milk.

Kate's stomach groaned. She hadn't been able to eat much yesterday with all that had transpired, but the smell of the hot bacon and steaming biscuits wafted beneath her nose and she pushed herself back up onto the bed.

Fannie set the tray on the night table and reached for the discarded wet towels, humming.

Wait. Humming?

Kate eyed her warily. What had happened to make the woman more cheerful than she'd been in a long while?

"I trust you slept well?" Fannie asked as she exchanged the damp pillow for another that had been sitting in the chair next to the window. "Mr. Deardon told me not to wake you, and to make sure you keep that foot elevated." She tsked. "Says you took a nasty fall last night."

Why was her cook taking orders from Noah?

"Fannie?"

"Yes, Miss Kate?"

"Where is Mr. Deardon now?"

"Why, he'd be out mending the porch railing." The older woman beamed. "He's a lovely man, Mr. Deardon. Already been to town and back this morning, collected all my eggs for me, talked with Virg and Oscar, and now he's working on the porch with Mr. Redbourne." She fluffed the pillow behind Kate's back and reached for the tray. "They're hard workers, those two."

"Where did they get the wood?"

"Mr. Mills dropped by first thing this morning with the load you had ordered."

Kate had wanted to build a new outbuilding at the edge of the east pasture for banding and branding season come February, and had figured it would be best to have it completed before the snow came.

"I appreciate all of this, Fannie, I do, but I cannot just lie here in my bedroom all day. There's work to be done."

"And it's getting done. Isn't that why you sent for a husband? To get help around here?" Fannie placed the tray over Kate's lap, the warmth filling her with unexpected anticipation.

"Yes, but…"

Mr. Thomas. She'd nearly forgotten the man.

"The other gentleman, the one who was here when we arrived home last night, where is he?"

The smile on Fannie's face quickly fell into one of disdain.

"That *gentleman*," her face contorted at the word, "is sitting in the kitchen in his fancy clothes, eating his 'mid-morning meal,'" she imitated him with a roll of her eyes, "and he tried to put his booted feet up on my table. I sure told him." She snatched up the wet pillow and topped it with the wet towels as she marched for the door. She turned back just before leaving. "I trust you'll make the right choice," she said smartly, then disappeared from view.

Kate couldn't remember how long it had been since she'd taken the time to eat a full breakfast. Normally, she grabbed a bite or two on her way out to work alongside the few hands who'd agreed to stay on after her father died. Dell, her father's best friend in Laramie and the ranch foreman, had convinced the men to stay out of respect. He'd even offered to marry her, but the older man was more like a distant uncle to her than a husband and she hadn't been able to bring herself to say yes.

It hadn't felt right. Still didn't.

Things had been a little awkward between them since.

She'd certainly learned a lot in the past few months about what it took to run a ranch this size, but she needed more help than what the foreman and the other three could provide. She needed a husband. There were a lot of hired hands willing to work for a male employer.

Dreams of falling in love and starting a family with the right man had given way to practicality, and so, she'd placed an ad that was supposed to reach several newspapers throughout the West. Dell hadn't taken to that idea so kindly. She was afraid she'd hurt his pride, but hoped he would understand. After all, he was more than twice her age and the ranch needed a man who didn't already have one foot in the grave.

Dell had been the foreman on the ranch since they'd moved to Laramie and he knew the business better than anyone she'd ever met, but even though she may not marry for love, she hoped to find a man that she could grow to love. Someone with whom she shared a connection. Someone who she could share her life with. Have a family with.

Maybe that man is Noah Deardon.

A smile danced with the corners of her mouth at the thought.

The pounding of the hammer on the porch ceased and Kate held her breath.

Would he come in here to see her?

She still wore the same men's work clothes she'd had on yesterday and could only imagine the state of her unkempt hair. When the hammering started again, she breathed out a heavy sigh of relief.

It didn't take long for her to finish up the hearty meal, followed by a fresh cup of milk to wash it all down. She wiped her hand across her face to remove any evidence that she may have dripped a little and set the tray to the side of the bed.

Her wardrobe sat only a few feet across the room. Even if she had to make the jump on one foot, she was determined to change her clothes. She may not be able to bathe in her current state, but at least she could wash her face, put on a clean dress, brush her hair, and look presentable.

Carefully, Kate removed the pillow from beneath her feet and shifted so that her legs dangled off the side of the bed. She put her good foot on the floor and reached for the wooden footboard for support. There were several feet between her bed and the wardrobe and nothing in between she could hold onto, so she stood up as tall as she could and hopped.

A couple of well-placed jumps landed her next to the closet. She could feel her heart beating in her foot, throbbing against her skin. She needed to get off of it, so she maneuvered herself into the chair sitting just opposite the wardrobe and sat down.

Heavy footfalls sounded in the hallway and stopped in front of her room.

Knock. Knock. Knock.

Kate swallowed hard. She wasn't sure what to say. "Come in," she squeaked, then cleared her throat.

The door opened and Levi stepped inside.

"What's wrong?" he asked.

She tried to push away her disappointment, but then Noah trailed in behind his cousin, a round, tin basin in his arms filled with water sloshing about. Kate's chest filled with sunshine at the sight of him and she sat up a little taller.

"Nothing," she finally answered with a simple shrug.

Fannie followed both men inside the room. Kate guessed she was acting as a chaperone. It was highly indelicate for an unmarried man to be in a woman's chambers, let alone two of them, but under the circumstances, she figured it could be overlooked. Just this once. Well, twice, if she counted last night.

Kate folded her lips together to hide the grin that threatened to spread across her face like a school girl with her first affection for a boy. She reached up to smooth her hair.

Why hadn't she asked Fannie for a brush when the woman was in her room earlier?

The moment Noah's eyes locked with hers, heat filled Kate's cheeks and the beat of her heart became a collection of rapid flutters. He walked toward her and sat the small tub down at her feet.

"How are you feeling this morning, Miss Callahan?"

Was it terribly improper that she wanted him to call her by her given name?

Kate.

"I'd be doing better with full use of both feet." Her attempt at humor faded with a half-hearted giggle turned into a whimper as he took her foot, lifted her leg over the edge of the washtub, and into the water.

"Oooooooo," she squealed. "That is freezing!" She yanked her foot from the ice-like liquid and shook her head.

Noah and Levi both laughed heartily.

"The faster the swelling goes down, the faster you'll be back on your feet."

Cold or not, she did not want to be constrained to stay in her bedroom for any longer than necessary. She had a ranch to run, a husband to choose, and a life to live. She plunged her foot back into the water and shivered as the chill ran up her back and down her arms.

"What's going on in here, then?" Mr. Thomas appeared in her doorway. "Don't we have a lot of work to get done today? I'd like to see the ranch, if you'd care to escort me, Miss Callahan."

Noah's jaw flexed. She guessed he wasn't very fond of the man either.

"I'll get Dell to show you the land and introduce you to the men," she said, leaning to see him through the Deardon-

Redbourne wall in front of her.

"Why can't *you* take me?"

Is he whining? Truly?

Kate had to consciously stop herself from rolling her eyes.

"Miss Callahan," Dell leaned in through the door.

It didn't seem like there had ever been this many people in her house at one time, let alone in the same room—*her* personal room, and it was becoming like a busy train station at departure time—crowded and stuffy.

"There is an older, quite distinguished looking gentleman here to see you, Katie," Dell said, his jaw flexing and his eyes narrowed. "Says he's here to make you his wife."

You have got to be kidding me.

Why did they just keep showing up? Her understanding was that in most situations like this, the men would correspond with the woman and then set up a time to meet. That's exactly how it was working with Mason Everett from Montana.

Four.

CHAPTER EIGHT

Noah closed his eyes at the news of yet another suitor come to call on Kate. He couldn't force himself to look up at her. They'd had a connection, he knew they had, so why was he so concerned about these other fellas?

"Who is he?" Kate asked Dell in disbelief.

"He said his name is a Mr. Gregory Stiles. From Boston."

"Boston?" Several of them repeated at the same time.

"That's what he said." Dell spat. "Boston."

"I got here first," Mr. Thomas announced, one finger in the air as if holding a place in line.

Everyone ignored him.

No, I got here first, Noah thought. But that didn't matter. What mattered was Kate. What she wanted. What she needed.

Noah could feel her eyes boring into the top of his head.

Maybe the man needed to see just what he was up against. He reached down for one of the dry towels that Fannie had brought in with her and gently lifted Kate's injured foot from the cold water he'd laced with chunks of ice he'd purchased in town this morning. He patted the limb dry, then got to his feet and reached down to pick her up off the chair.

"Let's go meet him," he said enthusiastically and started for the door. "Come on, Thomas."

"Wait! What?" Kate protested. "Put me down, Noah Deardon. Look at me."

He did as she asked before he could think better of it. Her eyes were wide, her expression worried.

Stop looking at me like that.

He liked the feel of her in his arms. Liked the way her chin jutted out defiantly. But when she looked at him with those eyes the color of honey, he would give her the world. Kate Callahan didn't know how beautiful she was and that endeared her to him even more.

"I can't meet a man in my parlor looking like this. I'd like to at least appear to be respectable. My hair must look like a bird's nest and I am hardly presentable in my da's button down shirt and men's trousers."

"I think you look downright appealing, Miss Callahan," Noah said as he gently set her down onto the bed, careful not to agitate her injury. "But, I'll do as you ask." He stood up tall and motioned toward the other two. "Levi, Mr. Thomas here, and I can go out and introduce ourselves, if you'd like."

Kate's face drained of color.

"Not without me, you won't!" she said, pushing herself to the edge of the bed and staring up at him defiantly.

He leaned down, his hands on his knees, his face so close to hers he could claim her lips with another inch. She didn't move, but her breaths became uneven, ragged.

"I wouldn't," he whispered, then stood up. "No matter how tempted I may be."

He liked seeing her a bit flustered.

Stop it, Deardon.

Jealousy never became a man. Though, it was nice to know he had some effect on her.

Noah was accustomed to being in control of…well, everything in his life. He could hear his Aunt Leah's voice now just as the last time he'd visited Redbourne Ranch.

The only person you can control is yourself, Noah Deardon. Do that well, and the rest will all work out as it should.

Levi's mama was a wise woman, the only mother figure Noah or his brothers had ever known.

"I'll just need a minute," Kate told him.

"Of course," he raised a brow and strode to the other end of the room. "We'll give you a moment."

Kate's exhale was audible. He glanced back at her and winked.

"Fannie," Kate called to the older woman, "would you stay and help me please?"

The men all stepped into the hallway, while Kate did whatever she needed to do in order to feel presentable.

Dell headed back out to the living area, presumably to tell the unsuspecting suitor that Miss Callahan would be out to greet him shortly.

Noah didn't move from his place in the hall.

"Well," Mr. Thomas slapped him on the shoulder, "this might prove to be more of a competition than I originally thought." He turned to follow Dell. "Time to step it up a notch, eh, Deardon?" he said with a haughty smirk.

Noah shoved his hands through his hair, rooted to his spot.

"Aren't you even the least bit curious?" Levi asked.

Noah had heard about wealthy businessmen back East who were looking to invest in or purchase successful ranches. He wanted to see this Mr. Stiles and vet him properly as much as anyone, maybe more, but something gave him pause.

"Of course, I am," he whispered louder than he'd intended. "But I gave her my word."

All this rigmarole complicated everything, not that he was afraid of a little competition. He needed to go about things a little differently."

"There is nothing for me to do except show Kate who I

am. To prove to her that I am the right man." He knew it sounded strange to want to be with a woman he'd barely met, but he wanted to spend the rest of his life getting to know her.

"How are you going to do that?"

Noah had been thinking long and hard about his plans.

What am I doing?

"This isn't me, Levi. If I am going to do this, I am going to do it my way."

He needed to show Kate that he was a man worth taking a risk over. He needed to court her, yes, but he also needed to convince her he was everything she'd asked for—

Hardworking? Check.

Knowledgeable of how to run a successful cattle ranch? Check.

Young and able-bodied. Mostly check. To some, his thirty years didn't qualify him as young, but he was still able-bodied.

Kind? Faithful? He tried. And check. To the end.

Now, Noah just needed Kate to get to know the real him and not the concocted version brought out by a trivial competition with several other potential suitors.

"I like the sound of that. What is your way?" Levi asked, leaning against the wall in the corridor.

"For starters, I'm going to work." Noah turned the opposite direction, heading for the back door.

There was a lot to be done. A ranch this size needed several more hired hands. Virg, Cal, and Oscar, along with Dell and Kate, had been doing a great job at maintaining some of the necessities, but a lot of the property had already started falling into disrepair, and it was simply too much for just the five of them to handle. At least with several potential suitors, more work would get done around the place.

Maybe.

Levi caught up to him as he stepped down off the back steps. "I'll do everything I can while I'm here." He stopped Noah and turned to face him. "I'm leaving at the end of next week. I've already been gone too long and the railroad needs me in Green River to oversee the men I sent ahead from Oregon."

"You recruited men from Oregon?"

"You didn't think you were the only one, did you?" Levi laughed. "What's the saying? Two birds, one stone. You were the one I wanted for Laramie. The only one." He clapped Noah on the shoulder. "Eamon's coming too. He's bought a place there and is trying to convince his daughter to join him. We'll head out on the seventh."

Noah knew the time would come when he'd have to say goodbye to his cousin. The man was key to the successful founding and civilization of several of the fledgling towns along the transcontinental route. Rather than encouraging the growth of the Hell on Wheels towns that plagued the growing railway, he brought respectability to the west by finding good folks to settle down and build their lives.

"Then, we'd better get to work."

CHAPTER NINE

Several days had passed since her accident, and Kate was itching to get out of the house. Since she couldn't walk the property, she figured she'd go for a ride to get some fresh air on this unusually warm November morning. Her foot still pained her, but the discoloration and swelling had all but disappeared except for some lingering stiffness. Noah had been faithful about making her soak it every night in the chilly water before she retired and so far, it seemed to be working.

She waited by the window until she saw the men leave for the hills with a few wagonloads of hay and wood to fix some of the broken fences, then grabbed the walking stick Noah had so kindly fashioned for her—most likely from a branch of the big white willow tree in the yard—and she made her way out to the stables. She'd heard the reports of what the small crew had been able to accomplish in the last few days, but she wanted to see it for herself. And to see each of the men who vied for her hand at work.

The extra help around the ranch had been a welcomed blessing, though she felt guilty that some would leave without getting what they'd come for.

A few of the outbuildings she'd wanted to have in place
before spring had already been completed, as had several wind
fences and snow barriers that would help protect the cattle
from harsh winter storms. And a giant open air barn, with only
a roof, but no walls, now towered over a good section of the
pasture just outside of the main corrals.

Many of the broken fences had been mended and three
new corrals had been erected in preparation of the new herd.
She'd only just received word yesterday that the drive had been
halted in Denver due to the imposing weather through the
wintery mountain passes.

A couple of the ranch hands had been left behind this
morning to repair tools, rebuild saddles, and tend to the milk
cows, for which Kate was grateful as she was able to convince
one of them to saddle her horse and help her mount.

"Thank you, Cal," she said with a smile.

The gruff old hand mumbled something back at her that
she didn't understand and walked away, shaking his head. She
guessed he didn't much care for being left behind. Well, she
understood that sentiment completely.

As she rode toward the east pasture, Kate looked up at the
beautiful mountainside that encompassed a good portion of
her property. The Callahans had been blessed to be some of
the first to settle the Laramie valley. Her father had chosen his
land well, with a large spring running through it and
mountainous terrain with an abundance of trees as well as
thick hearty meadows. She loved this land. Its beauty. She even
loved the smell of it—well, most of it. When she was away
from the vast numbers of cattle, the fresh scent of pine trees
and the crispness of the air renewed her. She pulled her mount
to a stop where she could glance over and appreciate the wide
expanse of her home.

Kate imagined that her herd from the last drive was being
auctioned off in Denver. She'd have to find another way to
secure the funds to purchase a few thousand more acres that

bordered her land if she was to expand her operations.

After a few awe-inspiring minutes, she shook out the reins and started moving again, riding along the ridgeline. She stopped a little ways up the trail when she noticed that one of the fences she and Cal had mended just last week had been knocked down again.

How had the others missed it? Kate made a mental note to have Dell swing back around and get it fixed before half the east herd escaped onto the open range.

She kept riding until she reached the corrals near the stone well in the northeast corner of her land where the men were supposed to be herding in and checking the health and well-being of the cattle that had come down to the low country a few days ago looking for food. She was pleased to see several more wind fences, a snow barrier, and a large slanted shelter had been constructed.

Bundles of hay had been strewn across the ground and a good hundred head had already been driven into the corral, but the men were nowhere to be seen. Either they were the fastest drovers she'd ever known or these cows had been here at least overnight.

Kate had been told of several sections of fence that were in need of mending along the property. Maybe the small, mismatched crew had already finished up here and moved along—though she doubted they'd been here at all or they would have fixed the downed section of fence a ways back. It was more likely they had started on the west side and were working their way east. She tugged her reins lightly to the left and leaned forward, nudging her mount toward the north side of the property.

It wasn't long before the sound of deep, male voices could be heard in the distance. She was close. As she curved around the little bend of the mountainside, the men came into view, but there were only three of them—Noah, Levi, and Mr. Stiles. There was no sign of Dell or Mr. Thomas.

Kate kept her distance, not wanting them to know she was there. A trail had been carved into the base of the mountain, leading up to an overhead lookout, hidden by trees. From that position, she may not be able to hear the conversation, but would be able to watch the men working and get a better feel for those who'd come to White Willow for the chance to own a part of it.

Luckily, she made it to the lookout without too much noise. She hadn't anticipated that the trees would block most of her view. The consequence for getting down from the horse would be that she wouldn't be able to get back up again, and without her walking stick, she'd either be stuck up here all night or have to tell them that she'd been spying. She opted to stay put and just make out what she could from behind the trees.

CHAPTER TEN

"Careful of that fence there, Stiles, it may get your suit dirty." Noah drew several of the large planks from the back of the wagon and carried them to the section of downed fence.

The fancy businessman shot to a standing position and brushed vigorously at his backside.

"I don't see why she doesn't just hire more ranch hands to do this kind of work." Gregory Stiles removed his white boater hat and wiped his forehead with the back of his wrist. "Once we're married, this type of labor will be a thing of the past. She'll be able to take tea with the other wives and…"

Noah stopped listening to the droll ramblings of the older man. It was obvious the Easterner was only there for a claim on White Willow. Having a wife that looked like Kate, however, would make him the envy of society.

They had left Dell and Clifford with the other wagon and supplies about a mile back to inspect the small group of Herefords that had wandered down from the high country and congregated in a small, grassy vale.

"So, we're leaving tomorrow," Levi said quietly, joining Noah with a bundle of nails.

Noah held the plank firmly in place against the top of the post still firmly planted in the ground and Levi drove three of the metal stakes through the wood. They repeated the process for the bottom edge and then Noah secured both sides with a string of wire, weaving them tightly against each other.

"Don't remind me. If I have to listen to one more story about how wonderful it is in the east without having someone to commiserate with, I may have to strangle him." He looked up at the man who now leaned against the edge of the wagon inspecting his fingernails.

If Kate was taken in by someone like Gregory Stiles, then she wasn't the kind of woman Noah believed her to be, nor someone he wanted to settle down with. Somehow, he knew that riches and glamour were not high on her list of priorities. She was nothing like his mother who had run off on her husband and four small children to pursue an opportunity to sing on some big, fancy stage.

As he headed back for the wagon, a splash of color caught his eye in the dense cluster of trees jutting out from the side of the mountain. He searched between the branches and locked eyes with Kate, watching them from above.

"We've got company," Noah said aloud, pointing up with his chin.

Levi's hand shot to his hip.

"Come on down, Kate!" Noah bellowed loud enough she would be able to hear him.

Mr. Stiles snapped his head toward the spot and immediately adjusted his black colonel tie. After a moment of quiet, the trees rustled and he could hear the horse's hooves as they headed away from them—Noah guessed there was a back trail that would lead her down to them.

It took several minutes, but Kate finally came into view from the east as she rounded the bend by the small watering hole.

He wondered how she had been able to get herself up

onto the horse and smiled at her ingenuity. When she'd lamented being cooped up in the house, Noah had gone out to the large white willow and found a broken branch, thick enough not to snap under her weight, but slender enough she could hold it in her hand. He'd sanded it smooth, carved her initials into it, and given it to her to help her get around the homestead.

From what Levi had told him, she was still a little wary on a horse, but by what he could see, she'd learned pretty quickly.

"What ya doing?" he asked in an exaggerated drawl.

She stared at him for a good while before answering.

"I wanted to watch y'all work and didn't think you'd let me come along—that you might think I'd just be in the way."

Honest. He liked that too.

"It's your ranch, Miss Callahan. You're welcome to go where you please."

Kate sat up straighter in the saddle. The smile she offered him filled his soul with fresh air.

"Hmhmmm." Mr. Stiles stepped toward her, bowed in half, holding his hat, and reached for her hand, bringing it to his lips.

"You are looking very lovely this morning, my dear. What a bright spot you've made on this ghastly day."

"Why, thank you, Mr. Stiles."

"I think he's full of 'ghas,'" Levi leaned in and whispered over his shoulder, imitating the man's slight accent.

Noah chuckled as he bent down and picked up several pieces of the broken fence panel.

"We're about finished here." He looked up at her and their eyes locked, nearly knocking the breath from him.

Stop it!

He glanced away as he tossed the wood into the back of the wagon to be used as fuel for the fire. "We'll just have to spread out the rest of this hay for the cattle and then we could accompany you back to the house. If you're willing to wait for a few minutes."

"That would be lovely." Kate dipped her head.

Mr. Stiles finally slid his hands into the gloves Noah had given him back at the house, his nose upturned, and walked over to pick up the last piece of the splintered fence, pinching it by the end with his thumb and forefinger. He raised it up, his lips curled into a grimace, and dropped it into the back of the buckboard, dusting his hands together as if he'd been slaving away all morning.

Noah rolled his eyes. He couldn't help it. The man was useless for any real ranch work.

"Come on."

Noah looked up to see Levi extending his arms up to help Kate down from the saddle.

"You've become quite a good rider, Katie. Your father would be proud. But, my guess is that your ankle is still sore enough, that you ought to ride in the wagon."

"I'll be fine," she said stubbornly.

"Come on," Levi said again, motioning with his raised hands that she needed to dismount.

A twinge of jealousy settled in Noah's gut as Kate swung her leg around the saddle horn and slid into his cousin's arms. He threw his tools into the back a little harder than he'd intended.

When Levi reached him, he held her out to Noah and winked. He gladly took the lovely Kate into his own arms, capturing her gaze momentarily before lifting her up onto the high seat. He met Levi's eyes with an unspoken 'thank you.' His cousin patted him on the shoulder and walked to the back of the wagon where he tied his mule-like gelding, then strode to the chestnut mare Kate had been riding and mounted.

There wasn't much Noah could do to make the ride more comfortable for her, as she would still have to rest her foot against the tilted plank in front of the seat, but he figured at least this way it wouldn't be wedged into a stirrup.

"Did you and the others come up through the west pass?" she asked when he joined her on the bench.

"Cal told us that there were a few scattered animals that had walked down into the ravine. Dell and Clifford are there checking on them now. Why? Is everything all right?"

"It might be nothing, but I noticed that one of the fences we mended last week is broken again and there are cattle corralled in the east pasture."

"How about I take you out there after supper and we'll have a look."

Kate nodded. "I'd like that."

She placed a hand on his forearm and Noah sucked in a breath.

"Thank you," she said with a smile that reached her eyes.

The ride back was pleasant and Noah found that he enjoyed her company even more than he'd remembered. Over the last several days he'd tried to keep his distance to give her room to breathe as she contemplated her decision—only seeing her when it was time to soak her foot and occasionally at mealtime.

He'd delved into the work, which made it a little easier, but he found that the more he got to know her, he wanted to spend more time with her. He selfishly would have loved to spend every waking moment with her. He was caught between all that needed to be done around the ranch and his desire to hear her laugh, to see the light in her eyes when she was pleased by something or someone.

No, keeping his distance would give the other two suitors vying for her affections plenty of rope to hang themselves as they stumbled all over each other to tell her how wonderful they were.

With only three ranch hands and the foreman, it was a wonder the White Willow Ranch still functioned. They'd lost nearly eight weeks' worth of work when more than a dozen ranch hands had up and left their employ to find work elsewhere after Emmett Callahan had been killed. So, Noah had pooled the help of all of the men available to him and together they'd been able to accomplish even more than he'd expected, regardless of Mr. Stiles' ineptitude.

When they got back to the homestead, the other wagon was already there. Noah jumped down off the seat and held his hands up for Kate.

She placed her hands on his shoulders and as he pulled her down into his arms, her face sat mere inches from his own. He glanced down at her perfectly shaped lips, imagining for a moment what it would be like to capture them with his own. He caught her eyes and stared at her for longer than was appropriate, but he could not deny the draw between them.

He groaned inwardly, his jaw flexing.

"You are beautiful," he whispered, surprised to hear that he'd said the words aloud, but pleased when color flooded her cheeks and a smile touched her lips.

"Are you two going to stand there all day staring at each other or are we going to get these horses unhitched from the wagon?"

Noah cleared his throat and breathed a laugh. "Coming," he called out in a two-note sing-song, then turned back to look at her.

"Go!" Kate told him. "I'll be fine from here. Just set me on the stairs."

Noah did as instructed and placed her down gently on the top step where she could hold onto the railing, then turned back to his chores. He led the horses and the wagon toward the barn. When he and Levi finally emerged from their tasks, they headed out toward the bunkhouse. Noah stole a glance at the veranda, biting back the disappointment that crept in at Kate's absence.

"Aaaaaaaa!" The shriek ended with a loud thud and a horse's whinny.

Noah and Levi scrambled in the direction from which the

scream had come. There, lying in a heap in front of one of the larger corrals, was Clifford, his horse running amuck, saddle straps and reins whipping about like lashes as the animal reared, pawing at the air, his eyes wide, and his ears pinned back against his head.

"Something's gotten under that horse's saddle," Noah said, looking for something that may have angered or spooked the gelding. It was the Arabian he'd met right after he'd arrived, only it was not acting like the same horse.

There was no sign of a skunk or raccoon, and it was too cold for a snake to be about. Nothing that would have spooked him.

Levi knelt down next to the man who'd been thrown from his mount.

"He all right?" Noah asked.

"Hey, Thomas," Levi called the man's name as he turned him over onto his back. His eyes were open, but there was no response.

"He's dead."

Noah looked down at the man whose neck was twisted at an awkward angle and unexpectedly Henry's face flashed through his mind as did the events of that horrible day just eight years ago—his big brother lying lifeless on the ground, his eyes open, blood oozing from his head.

No!

His gut contracted tightly as if he'd been punched hard, his heart wrenched in agony as he relived that life-altering moment, dropping to his knees, tears blurring his vision. He squeezed his eyes shut, gasping for air to fill his lungs.

Breathe, he coaxed, forcing the memories of his brother's death back into the locked chest where he'd hidden them a long time ago. With several deep, cleansing breaths, clarity returned and he bowed his head in thanks.

"Look, Noah, if this is going to be too hard for you..." Levi's hand clutched his shoulder in understanding.

Noah swallowed, wiped away wet streaks from his face, and pulled himself to his feet.

"I'm all right," he assured his cousin and then turned to the horse.

"I'll go get Doc Fulgrum," Cal called out.

"There's no need," Noah told him quietly.

Cal's eyes grew wide and his head jerked toward the dead man.

Noah exchanged glances with Levi, who heaved the dead man up into his arms and carried him to the house.

"We need to calm this horse before anyone else gets hurt," Noah said firmly. "Do you understand?"

The hired hand swallowed, then nodded.

"Good." He nodded too, then turned to the beautiful light-colored steed. "Whoa," Noah called softly as he held up his hands, stepping toward the distraught horse.

The Arabian tossed his head back and forth, bucking and twisting awkwardly, snorting a warning at Noah to not get any closer.

The front door clacked against the frame as it shut. A gentleman with broad shoulders and graying hair stepped out onto the porch with Kate tucked under his arm, her hand covering her mouth. Their eyes locked for a brief moment, but when the gentleman started down the stairs with her, Noah held up his palm to stop them. He needed to focus and he couldn't do that if he was worried about Kate.

"Stay back," he cautioned.

The older gentlemen set Kate down on the steps and it took everything Noah had inside of him to ignore how the soft blue dress she wore clung to her very feminine curves, and her newly brushed hair cascaded down her shoulders and across her chest.

Focus, Deardon!

The Arabian bucked again.

It had been a long time since he'd seen a horse act so

erratically. Something was off. He glanced at the horse's feet, but by the way he pranced about, there was no sign of injury to his legs. A red, sticky-looking splotch appeared just below the ridge of the saddle, oozing down from the underside of the blanket.

He is hurt.

In moments, Dell, Eamon, Levi, and the three hired hands had joined him, forming a semi-circle around the mount, ropes at the ready.

The steed reared, screeching.

"We need to get that saddle off of him," Noah declared emphatically.

"You are a blamed fool, Deardon, if you think you're going to be able to get close enough to that mount to remove his saddle." Dell snorted.

You've met this horse, Deardon. Let him know he can trust you.

"Levi," he called quietly. "Go to the barn and get the bag of apples from my saddle bags."

Noah continued to watch the horse, trying to figure out the best way to calm the animal and appeal to his better nature.

"Enough of this." Dell pulled out his rifle and aimed.

Click. Click. Click.

Levi stood behind the man, having returned quickly from his task, his newly cocked pistol aimed at the foreman's head. "I wouldn't," he said as he handed Noah the fruit.

If shooting a horse without finding a cause for its behavior was the foreman's approach to ranching, he was in the wrong profession.

Noah nodded his appreciation at Levi as he opened the bag.

Dell dropped the rifle to his side and Levi re-holstered his weapon.

"Whoa, big fella," Noah said, placing one of the apples in his palm as he had last night and then he tucked another under his arm. "It's all right." He took a step toward the horse, the other hand raised lightly, his fingers waving in a downward motion. "I can't help you, boy, if you won't let me." He spoke soothingly to the fitful Arabian.

The horse neighed and took a few steps backward.

Noah broke his eye contact and dropped his head, inviting the steed closer.

Nature's silence descended on the ranch as everyone stood around them, watching. The horse stopped kicking about and, for the moment, stood perfectly still, except for his irregularly swishing tail. He tousled his head, but didn't shy away as Noah got closer.

Amazed, he held out the apple and waited, breathing slowly, but deeply. The horse sniffed at the treat, then wrapped his lips around it and took a bite. When it was gone, Noah took a side step toward the saddle, but the Arabian backed away several short steps, still wary of assistance.

"What should we call you, boy?" he asked, almost in a whisper. He'd never learned Mr. Thomas's name for the mount and thought it a shame.

What a magnificent animal.

The horse dipped his head and sniffed at the air.

"Do you want another one?" He retrieved the apple from under his arm and placed it in his palm, repeating the process.

This time, Noah backed away a few feet and sat down on the ground, facing the guarded horse, but giving him his space.

He waited in silence as did the small, anxious crowd.

After several minutes, the beautiful animal took a step toward him, then another, until he dropped his head level with Noah's.

"Good boy," he said, reaching out to rub the horse's nose, grazing over the bridle as he grasped a hold of the slack reins.

Noah moved his attention to the neck as he pulled himself into a standing position and maneuvered to the horse's flank. He quickly unbuckled the rear cinch and let it hang while he moved to the front, cautiously draping the fender and stirrup up over the saddle as he folded the tie strap.

When it was time to remove the saddle, Noah grabbed ahold of either end of it. The Arabian was tall, standing at least fourteen hands, so he was careful not to slide the tack from the horse's back as he lifted. He handed the saddle to Levi and reached for the blanket. There was a distinct bump in the wool covering directly above the blood that now stained the light coloring of the horse. He eased the blanket backward away from the horse's hide and only when it stuck did the steed start to fidget. Noah slowly pulled a little harder, peeling back the cloth to reveal a full stem of thick, dark brown burrs embedded into flesh, drawing blood.

He exchanged glances with Levi.

"How did an experienced horseman, like Clifford Thomas claimed to be, not know there were burrs attached to the underside of his saddle blanket?" Noah shook his head as he reached down slowly to pull the knife from the sheath in his boot. "Unless…"

"Someone else saddled his mount," Levi finished his thought.

Why would someone want to hurt a man so new to town? Whatever the answer, Noah knew he needed to protect Kate. If someone were trying to sabotage the ranch, then she was in as much danger as any of them. If not more.

Noah eased the blade of the knife beneath the prickly thorns and eased them out of the horse's hide. Once the nuisance had been removed, the Arabian shook his head and nickered quietly. He moved in a circle, nudging Noah's armpit.

Noah laughed, realizing he was looking for another apple.

Levi handed him the bag.

"Who did this to you, boy?" he asked, remembering the conversation he'd had with Kate on the way home about one of the fences on the east side of the property being down and cattle being corralled. Something was definitely off and someone at the ranch had a lot of explaining to do. He just needed to find the culprit and put a stop to his plans.

"Noah," Levi started, "if someone here did this on purpose—"

"I know. The stakes just got a whole lot steeper."

CHAPTER ELEVEN

"Not quite the type of excitement I'd hoped to find at a well-respected ranch like White Willow," Mr. Stiles told Nate, who'd taken over responsibilities as sheriff.

Noah and Levi wrapped up poor Mr. Thomas's body in a grey sheet tied off with rope over several locations on his body and lifted him atop the undertaker's canvas stretcher that had been laid out on the floor in front of the couch.

Kate had seen too much death—enough to last anyone a lifetime—and she was disheartened at the thought of anyone dying alone, without someone to mourn their passing. She was saddened that she didn't know whether or not Clifford Thomas had any kin or friends to grieve his loss.

"What did you know about this Mr. Thomas?" Nate asked, his broad shoulders pulled back as he stood at his full height. His dark hair, sprinkled with grey flecks, had been cut short, and a toothpick protruded from his mouth. He tilted his head with a crack, then began pacing in front of her and Dell, one eye half shut as he looked at them.

"Only that he's from Abilene," Kate volunteered from her seat in the rocking chair next to the cool hearth, "but he'd

been working as a drover on a cattle drive through Colorado."
She didn't know what else she could tell the new lawman. "He
only just arrived a few days ago," she told him.

"Why was he here? Was he staying here, Kate? At White
Willow?"

She looked down at the floor. It wasn't her fault Mr.
Thomas was dead. Was it?

Dell handed Nate a copy of the Boulder Chronicle
newspaper with the ad she'd placed, and stabbed a finger at the
precise spot it was located, nearly tearing the paper from the
sheriff's hands.

How did he get that?

Nate pulled the newspaper down, away from him to read
the fine-sized print. Then, after scanning the ads, his gaze shot
up at Kate.

"This true?" he asked. "You looking for a husband?"

"Well," she glanced over at Noah, arms folded, eyes
scrunched together and staring at the sheriff, "yes, sir."

Nate looked over his shoulder and stepped back as if
noticing Noah, Levi, and Eamon for the first time.

"Walker," he stepped toward the trio, nodded at Eamon,
and held out his hand. "Levi," he offered the same courtesy.
When he stood in front of Noah, the handsome would-be
suitor stood up tall and held out his hand.

"Noah Deardon, Sheriff."

"Didn't I see you last week after the hanging?"

Noah nodded.

Kate's gut twisted at the memory of the deputy marshal
hanging from the rafters in that cabin.

He can't hurt you anymore, she echoed the sentiments she'd
shared with Stella. Or anyone else.

It seemed like ages ago that she'd seen the man
responsible for her father's death hanging from the rafters of
that cabin, and was surprised that she'd hardly thought about
him since...since...Noah arrived at White Willow.

"New in town?" Nate took the toothpick out of his mouth with one hand and shook Noah's hand firmly with the other.

"Yes, sir."

"Are you here to marry Miss Callahan?"

"Yes, sir," he said without hesitation.

Kate warmed inside, heat rising in her cheeks. She barely knew the man, but he had all the right things to say.

Nate's eyes opened almost as wide as his mouth, as if he hadn't quite believed it when it was written in black and white right in front of him.

"Wouldn't you give up your home to move across the country for a chance to marry such a beautiful and smart woman who had offered to share her life, and her ranch, with you? Even if she couldn't walk right for a bit?" Noah added, glancing over at her with a wink. "Frankly, I'm surprised that half the men in the territory aren't trying to court her."

Kate's insides turned to gelatin. He had to stop doing that.

"Hmhmmm." Mr. Stiles, moved his lean and lanky form quickly between the sheriff and Noah. "Yes, you see, Sheriff," he said, "that is exactly what I have done." He placed a hand on Nate's shoulder, turned him toward the kitchen, and walked next to him as if sharing a secret.

Kate could still hear every word from her position on the couch.

"Well, not *move* exactly, but marry the girl and share the responsibility of her ranch, absolutely."

Kate rolled her eyes. She didn't know why a businessman from Boston had any desire to 'share the responsibility of her ranch.' And he'd made it abundantly clear that he was only here for the property.

She dared another glance at Noah, who glowered at Mr. Stiles with his arms folded and his brows scrunched together.

"I am ready for the deceased," Mr. Dixon announced as he took a step inside the open doorway.

Noah and Eamon picked up the wooden handles of the stretcher poles and solemnly followed the undertaker out to his carriage, followed by Levi and Dell.

Kate pushed herself into a standing position, keeping her injured foot from touching the floor, and used the furniture and walls to help maneuver the room. Just as she reached the front door, Nate came up behind and then around in front of her, standing in the entryway, crooking his arm.

Nate Boswell had befriended her family when they'd first arrived in Laramie and had been good to them ever since. She accepted his kind offer and hopped out onto the porch with him.

"What happened to your foot?" he said, glancing out, into the distance.

Kate did not want to tell him how she'd made a fool of herself, ogling Noah Deardon, so she skipped the details.

"Porch railing broke. I fell. Simple as that."

When they reached the top step, heat rose again in her cheeks. The railing had not only been mended, but the entire set of steps and handrail had been completely refinished.

"You getting along all right?"

"I've had a lot of help."

"I can see that," Nate raised a brow.

Kate hit his arm playfully.

"Mary will want to come by and check in on you. Maybe bring you some of her sweet potato pie."

"Fannie's been very good to me, but you know how I love Mary's cooking. I would enjoy the delicacy. Thank you."

"I don't know if it's delicate, but it sure goes a long way to filling a man's belly." He laughed loudly. "And a woman's," he added with a grin.

Silence passed between them as they watched the men load the body into the back of the hearse.

"You okay with all these fellas staying here at the ranch?"

"I know how to take care of myself, Nathaniel."

After her father died, Nate and Dell had taken it upon themselves to teach her how to shoot, along with a few other basic skills that would help her out here on the range. She'd learned how to find water and dig a well, how to skin and clean a deer—a chore she hoped she'd never have to do again—and how to hitch a team of horses to the wagon. She'd been a quick learner.

"I know you consider yourself quite an independent woman. We just worry about you being out here all on your own."

"I'm not alone. And I'll be married soon."

"I'm glad you're aching to get married. Marriage is good for the soul." He looked down at the men standing in the yard. "So, which one of these lucky fellas gets your hand?" he asked with a knowing smile.

"I haven't decided yet."

"Kate Callahan, it is as plain as the nose on your face who you want to choose." He nudged her shoulder against the wooden pillar at the top of the stairs. "Don't think I haven't seen the way you look at that Deardon fella."

Is it that obvious?

"The Harvest Jubilee is next week," she told him. I've decided I have until then to make a decision."

Nate laughed.

"And you're actually considerin' that easterner?" He snorted another disbelieving laugh. "You're not blind, woman, and you have a good head on your shoulders. You'll make the right choice. Just let me know when I can congratulate Deardon." He left her leaning against the pillar and ran his hand down the new railing.

How does he do it?

He whistled.

"That's some fine workmanship," he said, rubbing the wood. "Whose is it?" he asked with a grin.

Kate squinted at him. She knew he was teasing, but she

wanted to wipe the smirk right of Nate Boswell's face. He knew exactly who had mended the railing.

With another chuckle, he descended the rest of the stairs to join the men at the large, black hearse.

She glanced up at Noah, who caught her looking at him and smiled warmly, raising his hand in a brief wave, before turning back to his conversation.

"Glad we are finished with that nasty business." Mr. Stiles came up to stand right behind her. "Miss Callahan, if I may have a moment of your time."

She wasn't sure how to tell the man that she'd already decided that he was no longer being considered for the position as her husband.

"Mr. Stiles, I appreciate your travelling all the way out to Laramie, but—"

"I've had quite enough of living out here in such cramped quarters and until we are married and I can join you inside the house, I will be staying the night in town at the Grand Oak Hotel. I wondered if you might join me for some supper this evening at the restaurant there." He took her hand in his and raised it to his lips.

Kate pulled her hand away slowly, irritated that the man had completely cut her off.

"Mr. Stiles, as I was saying before, I think it would be best if—"

"I'll just accompany the sheriff. If this town is going to be one of my homes, I would like to get acquainted with the people in it." He said, placing his white boater hat on his head as he turned to go down the stairs.

He did it again!

"I am *not* going to marry you, Mr. Stiles!" she screamed what she'd been thinking almost since the moment he'd arrived.

Everyone fell silent and turned to look up at her. Once again, heat seared her cheeks and she closed her mouth in an apologetic smile.

If he'd only let her get a word in edgewise, it would have saved them both the embarrassment.

"Yes, well…" Mr. Stiles didn't finish his sentence, just removed his hat with a short bow, and hustled down the rest of the steps and out to the barn, where she suspected his horse had already been saddled and waiting.

Mr. Dixon also lifted his hat toward her from his perch atop the hearse, then slapped the reins, turned his black wagon around, and headed out through the gate.

The others returned to their discussion without a word to her, but Kate didn't miss the smile that briefly touched Noah's lips.

Mr. Stiles emerged from the barn a few moments later in a small, uncovered carriage pulled by a single Appaloosa.

Of course.

Kate watched him until he reached the peak of the hill that would take him down into town. A larger, black carriage crossed his path, which Kate recognized immediately as Reverend Jones's.

It wasn't long before she could make out that it was not the good Reverend in the carriage, but his wife, Cindy, Nate's wife, Mary, and Ingrid Fulgrum, the doctor's wife. She could only imagine what the women would think of her allowing perfect strangers to bunk at the ranch along with the hired hands with only Fannie as a chaperone.

As the ladies pulled in through the wooden archway at the front of the yard, Nate and Dell went to greet them, while Noah and Levi joined her on the porch.

"Looks like you've got company," Levi stated the obvious.

Kate was grateful she'd chosen to wear a dress today instead of the work trousers and button down shirt she usually donned on a work day. The last thing she needed was for the three most respected ladies in town to think she was a heathen. While all of the women were near her age, they were already married. Mary and Ingrid both had little girls and the latter was expecting.

"Kathryn," Ingrid greeted her as if she were the wise matron of the group, though she was the youngest of all of them.

"It's Kate," she reminded her politely through the smile hiding the grit of her teeth.

"Oh, yes. Of course. Kate," Ingrid corrected as she held out a basket covered in red and white checked gingham and leaned down to give her a sort of half hug.

"Thank you."

"What is Mr. Dixon doing here? Is everything all right?"

"No. There's been an accident."

"Who is it?" Ingrid asked, bringing her white glove-covered fingers up to her mouth.

"Clifford Thomas," Kate responded matter-of-factly.

"Who?" Ingrid asked again.

"A man from Abilene, here on…business." How else could she describe his purpose here? She glanced at Cindy who had been the only person she'd confided in when she'd placed the ad.

"Hi, Kate." Cindy nodded, waving from the step below as she handed Kate a slender white paper bag around Ingrid. "Are you all right? He wasn't…" Cindy's question trailed, but Kate understood.

Kate shook her head.

Cindy was the oldest of them at twenty-four and had been the closest thing Kate'd had to a real friend in town. It had only been a few months since the girl had married the preacher and their friendship just hadn't been the same since. She looked happy, though. That was all that mattered.

The reverend had just been offered a job with a small parish in Montana and they would be moving soon. Kate had been saddened to hear the news.

She lifted the bag and sniffed the delicious scent rising

from its contents.

"Is this what I think it is?" Her tongue touched her lips in anticipation as she opened the top of the petite package. The sweet, buttery aroma that arose from the bag in a wave tickled Kate's nose with its surprising warmth.

Cindy was a wonderful cook and had recently discovered the art of candy-making. Several large pieces of warm golden toffee had been wrapped and placed carefully inside the bag.

"Why, Mrs. Jones," Kate said excitedly, deliberately using the woman's married name, "they look simply delightful."

Cindy beamed at her, obviously pleased by her appraisal.

Mary finally joined them, her arms held out with what Kate guessed was a sweet potato pie covered in a blue and green striped cloth. By what Nate had said, Kate thought the woman was going to stop by sometime later in the week or even the next, but Mary had always had a keen intuition for knowing the precise moment to call.

"I'm so sorry to hear about this Mr. Thomas person," Mary said with a frown. "I understand he's been helping out around the ranch."

Kate brushed her hand across her skirt, hoping to smooth out the wrinkles. She rested Ingrid's basket on the porch with Cindy's toffee on top and took the pie with a gracious smile.

"If you must know…" She hated to tell them the real reason Mr. Thomas had been there, but they would find out sooner or later and she figured it would come better from her. "He was here in response to an advertisement I placed in the newspaper. For a husband," she finished her sentence without remorse.

Cindy smiled sympathetically, but the other two's eyes opened as wide as saucers and their jaws dropped unbecomingly.

"You what?" Ingrid was the first to recover. "But, why? You're so…so…"

"Perfect," Cindy finished for her.

"Yes, well, of course that's what I meant."

Kate recounted her reasons for requesting a 'mail-order-husband' and informed them that Noah was at White Willow for the same reason.

When Cindy looked at her with raised brows, Kate nodded.

"Excuse me, ladies." All of a sudden, Noah was standing there as if just by thinking his name, he would appear.

He climbed the stairs and took the pie from Kate's hand, then reached down for the gingham covered basket. He took them inside the house and returned with two more chairs to add to those already situated on the porch behind the veranda railing, then handed her the walking stick.

As the ladies each took a seat, Noah held out his arm for Kate. She slipped her hand into the open space and, with his help, hopped to the chair he'd brought out for her. Once she was situated, he descended the stairs and rejoined the men, still in deep conversation.

"You *must* tell us everything," Cindy said with a smile.

It had been a long time since Kate'd had a woman around, at least a woman her age she could talk to, confide in. She missed it. Fannie was great, but it wasn't the same. She told the girls about everything that had happened, including how she'd damaged her ankle falling through the railing. They were a perfect audience, ooooing and aaahhing in all the right places.

"Oh, I nearly forgot." Ingrid handed her a sealed letter with a postmark from Montana. "The postmaster asked me to deliver this to you."

"Is that from the gentleman who's been corresponding with you?" Mary asked excitedly.

Kate hadn't received a letter from Mason Everett in a couple of weeks.

"Well, aren't you going to open it?" Ingrid coaxed.

Her hands shook as she turned the envelope over. In their last correspondence he'd mentioned his desire to come to

White Willow and meet her in person, but she'd been hesitant, wanting to know more about him before taking that leap. She realized now, that the best way to get to know a person was to talk with them, face to face, to observe how they interacted with others, to spend time with them.

"I'll be right back," she said as she pushed herself into a standing position and reached for her walking stick. She could probably have managed without it, but she liked the feel of it in her hand, knowing Noah had made it just for her.

"Can I help you?" Cindy asked, pushing her chair backward in an attempt to stand.

"I'll be fine. Just give me a moment." As much as Kate appreciated everyone's help, she hated being dependent on other people and knew the more she did on her own, the more she would be able to do.

With the aid of the giant stick, Kate made it inside the house and to her bedroom, without incident, where she kept a small box of Mr. Everett's letters hidden in the back of the drawer in the night table next to her bed. She retrieved it, along with the letter opener sitting adjacent to her pen and stationary.

With a little effort, she tucked the box under her arm and made her way back out to the veranda where the others sat, chatting quietly. She set the box on the short tea table, glancing out into the yard. The intense conversation between the men had apparently been adjourned or they had taken it elsewhere as she couldn't see a single one.

"What's this," Mary asked, reaching into the box, pulling out a few letters, and letting them slip back out of her fingers. "Are all these from him? From *Mason*?" She asked as though using his given name was something forbidden and wicked.

Kate nodded.

The women all scrambled to retrieve Mr. Everett's messages to her. As they read about the man's life and what he hoped for in a wife, their hands migrated to their hearts and mouths. No one would have ever guessed that she was the lone spinster in the group.

"Are you sure Mr. Everett doesn't have a chance?" Ingrid asked after reading aloud the last note Kate had received before today. "He sounds like such a lovely man."

Cindy and Mary both nodded their heads in agreement.

Over the last couple of months, Kate had looked forward to the arrival of each new letter. Mason Everett had seemed like the perfect man on paper, but the idea of perfect and the real thing—flesh and blood—were two very different things.

Noah Deardon was the right man for her. And this ranch.

Finally, she could admit it to herself. Somehow she'd known it all along, but it hadn't seemed real. Noah hadn't seemed real. He was exactly what she'd dreamed the man who answered her ad would be. Exactly what she wanted and needed in a husband. While she'd been incapacitated for the better part of a week, he had put his head down and gotten to work on the things that needed doing around the place. If it hadn't been for his expertise and knowhow, White Willow would be no better off today than it was three months ago.

He was real. Very real.

"Aren't you going to open it?" Mary asked.

"I'm dying to know what Mr. Perfect has to say next," Ingrid added.

"Why Ingrid Fulgrum, you are a happily married woman," Cindy playfully chastised.

"Married," she responded with a raised brow. "Not dead."

The three visiting women all laughed.

Kate picked up the last envelope in one hand and the letter opener in another. Slowly, she sliced open the top, unsure why she'd been suddenly washed over with apprehension. She placed the sharp metal instrument down on the table and pulled the linen paper from its case.

With a slow, deep breath, she unfolded the letter, cleared her throat, and began to read.

Dear Miss Callahan,

I hope my letter finds you in good spirits. Thank you for your lovely note. I appreciate you opening up your heart to me with the struggles you are facing on the ranch. I'll be there within a fortnight. I know you said to wait, but I feel it necessary to get there in time to help you with the winter preparations. I look forward to our meeting.

With admiration,
Mason Everett

"A fortnight?" Kate turned over the envelope to look at the postmark and calculated the days since it was sent. "That's tomorrow." She dropped her hand with the letter down into her lap.

"How exciting," Mary said, clapping her hands.

How was she going to tell Noah about the letters? About Mr. Everett?

"What am I going to do?" she asked, looking at Cindy for answers.

The preacher's wife scooted her chair closer to Kate and put a reassuring hand on her knee. "You'll figure something out."

Kate caught glimpse of Noah leaving the bunkhouse with a large leather satchel, heading toward the stables. She sat up a little taller in her chair to get a better look over the railing. She leaned forward slightly, squinting her eyes. Her heart thumped in her chest and dread filled her mind.

He can't be leaving. Can he?

Not now. Not after she'd realized he was the one she wanted to stay.

"Excuse me for a moment," Kate said, not taking her eyes off of Noah until he disappeared inside the wooden structure.

She stood. Taking the steps one at time, she made it to the bottom, hobbled across the yard with scarce use of her stick, and swung the stable door open wide.

"Are you leaving?"

CHAPTER TWELVE

Noah walked into a room of chaos. Beds had been upended, drawers pulled out of the dressers, and the table, with its several chairs, had been knocked over. Someone had tossed the bunkhouse, but what had they been looking for? And had they found it?

He shook his head and breathed out an exasperated sigh before bending over and picking up the overturned table and righting the chairs.

Who would've had access to the building in the last few hours? The list wasn't very long and Noah had his suspicions. He arranged the mattresses back on their bedframes and as he walked between two of the beds to return the drawers to their places, the floor beneath him creaked loudly.

He stepped away from and back onto that section of the floor, adding a little bounce as he stepped, then dropped to his knees, feeling for any indication that there may be a hidden chamber beneath the floor. He discovered a divot in one of the boards and slid his fingers along the ridge, pulling as he went. The end plank lifted to reveal a large, brown leather satchel jammed inside of a hollowed out cavern.

Noah glanced over his shoulder to make sure no other eyes were on him as he lifted a few more boards and pulled the bag from the concealed cavity in the ground. He threw back the top flap and a dozen paper bills floated out. He grabbed them, shut the satchel and quickly returned the floorboards to their secured position.

Levi and Eamon were still out in the stable preparing for their trip to the newly established rail station in Green River—loading their saddle bags and securing their tack. Of course, they only had to ride as far as the rail depot in Laramie and then load their horses and bags onto the train when it came through.

Too bad the sheriff had left with the undertaker. But it was a good thing Eamon was a Pinkerton and good at his job. He would be able to help them get to the bottom of all the recent troubles at the ranch.

Noah picked up the bag and headed for the door, scanning the yard for any prying eyes, before venturing out toward the stable.

"Just about done in here," Levi said as he looked up in greeting.

Noah set the satchel down on the work table. "Are we alone?" he asked quietly.

"What are you talking about?" Levi asked, but with one glance at Noah's face, his playful smile fell. "Eamon?" he called for his friend and the man popped his head out from the stall his horse had been staying in. "Come on out here." Levi turned back to Noah. "What is it?" he asked, nodding toward the satchel.

Noah picked it up and turned it on end.

Ching. Ching. Ching.

Gold and silver coins of all shapes and sizes spilled out onto the table accompanied by hundreds of dollars in paper bills. Several rolled pieces of parchment and a leather-bound folder also fell to the counter.

"What is all this?" Eamon asked, an eyebrow raised at Noah, joining them at the work table.

"I found it hidden under the floorboards in the bunkhouse. Somebody had ransacked the place looking for it." He turned to Eamon. "I thought we might be able to find something that will help us figure out what is going on around here. It's too much of a coincidence that Thomas died this morning and he's got all this money stashed away."

Eamon picked up the leather folder and opened it.

"There must be a dozen papers of cattle ownership in this folder. And..."

"What?"

"A deed. To White Willow," he said, pointing at the ground. "It is signed by Clifford Thomas and...Kate Callahan."

Levi and Noah exchanged glances.

A nagging feeling sat in the pit of Noah's stomach. He just couldn't believe that she would choose Thomas over him. Wouldn't believe it.

"It's a forgery," Eamon stated nonchalantly—as if Noah's whole world didn't depend on it.

"How can you tell?" Levi asked while Noah caught his breath.

"That's not Kate's writing." He pointed at her signature. "I have seen enough of her lists of supplies she made me pick up in town to tell you that I know what her scribbling looks like, and that is not it." He picked up a chunk of metal from the table. "It wouldn't be legal anyway until he had a notary's stamped seal." He held up the authentic looking notary stamp.

Noah unrolled the closest parchment to him. There, staring back at him, was a picture clear as day of none other than Clifford Thomas, the word WANTED written in huge letters across the top. He turned it around to show the others.

"No wonder someone wanted him dead," Eamon said loudly. "I knew I'd seen that fella somewhere before. He's been thieving cattle all across the west."

The scratching sound of the stable doors as they swung wide had Noah scrambling to re-roll the parchment and cover the money with the oversized satchel.

"Are you leaving?" Kate's voice had a hint of anger mixed with confusion.

He spun around to face her.

"Kate," Noah said, recognizing too late his informality. "What are you doing out here? Don't you have guests?"

"Are you leaving?" she demanded again.

"Not unless you're giving me the boot." He tried to appear calm, but he didn't know what to do with his hands, so he stuck them firmly into his pockets.

Her face relaxed and she exhaled loudly, her relief visible.

The sound of the coins scratching against the table and clanging against each other was hard to miss. Noah closed his eyes. He didn't want to keep anything from Kate—especially something that could be putting her and her entire ranch in danger.

"Listen, Miss Callahan, we need to talk."

"Yes, we do." Before he could say another word, she took a step inside the stable. "A gentleman who has been writing to me for several weeks has just written to inform me that he is coming to White Willow."

That was the last thing he had expected her to say and it took him completely off guard.

Slow down, Deardon, he told himself as he struggled to gather his thoughts. And his emotions.

He waited, staring at her for a moment before he trusted himself enough to speak.

"Thank you for letting me know." He didn't want to wait anymore. Didn't want to keep wondering if she'd felt the same connection between them as he had. "Are you interested in him?" He wanted to smack his forehead against the palm of his hand. "What I mean to ask, is…"

"I thought he was the perfect suitor. He said all the right things in his letters and had the experience and intelligence that I was looking for when I first placed the ad."

"I see." He swallowed, unsure he wanted to hear anymore. "Well, I…"

"If you'll just let me finish," she said, reaching out and brushing her fingers against the flesh of his arm.

He wanted so badly to pull her into his arms, tell her that was where she belonged, and to taste the sweetness of her kiss, but he rooted his feet to the ground and flexed his jaw in restraint.

"I realized that everything I knew about him were from words on a page. And everything I know about you is from talking to you, watching you…being with you."

"So, what are you saying?" He wanted to be sure he understood the meaning in her words.

"Are you going to make me say it?" she asked with a smile. "Yes."

"It's you, Noah Deardon. You are the one I want. I don't care who else comes knocking at our door. I've made my choice."

His heart flipped inside.

Our door.

She'd made her choice. He should be jumping up and down, knowing she would be his, but something was missing.

Love.

Levi cleared his throat.

Noah had almost forgotten that he and Eamon were still behind him.

"This is great and all, but do you think this conversation could wait?" Eamon asked from behind him.

Kate's brows scrunched with concern.

Noah nodded. "Eamon's right. Look, Kate…"

Her jaw tensed and her chin lifted.

"I have to tell you something. And you're not going to like

it."

Kate took a step backward, literally bracing herself against the stable's doorframe. She stared at him, the catch-lights in her eyes wet. He took the two steps that separated them and placed his hands on her shoulders, looking down into her honey-colored eyes, her emotions as transparent as glass.

She shook her head as she turned on her heel, escaping his touch, and started back for the house, faster than he would have thought her able with a sprained ankle.

"Well," Levi said in a 'you're-such-a-dolt' sort of way, "go after her."

"Miss Callahan," Noah called as he followed her outside of the stable. "Where are you going?"

She didn't pause even for a moment, but still limped as quickly as she could toward the house and the ladies sitting on the veranda.

"Katie Callahan!" he yelled. "I love you!"

She froze and slowly turned around to face him. The women on the veranda stood and Noah could hear the crunching of gravel behind him. They had an audience.

He closed the distance between them in a few heartbeats, delving his hands into her dark brown tresses, and bracing the back of her head as he lifted her face to meet his kiss. He didn't care who watched. Kate would be his wife as soon as they could get the pastor and he needed her to know how he felt.

He'd waited long enough and didn't want anything standing in the way of their new life together. He deepened the kiss, dropping his hands so his arms could wrap all the way around her and pull her in tightly to him. He groaned softly when her hands slid up his chest and around his neck, her fingers grasping the hair at the back of his neck and holding him in place as she readily returned his affection.

Well aware of their spectators, Noah broke the kiss, but did not release his hold around her as he bent down to look into her eyes. Wet trails lined her face and his gut churned at the thought that he'd put them there.

"Now that we've got that settled, can I talk to you?"

Kate bit her lip and nodded. "Just let me say goodbye to the girls."

He kissed the tip of her nose, then lifted her into his arms and carried her up the porch steps, setting her down in front of the table where the ladies awaited with appreciative smiles. Noah was glad these women seemed like real friends and not like so many of the busy-bodies he'd encountered back home. The last thing he wanted was for her to be the talk of the town for a simple kiss.

Who was he kidding? It had been an incredible, delectable kiss.

Cal had already hitched the carriage the women had arrived in and had it waiting for them as they descended the stairs with a wave. Mrs. Jones, the pastor's wife, hugged Kate tightly and whispered something in her ear before leaving.

Once the women pulled out of the drive, Noah leaned down to pick her up again.

"I can walk, you know."

"I know," he said as he pulled her back up into his arms and headed back toward the stable, past Levi and Eamon who both stood there grinning, the satchel strung over Eamon's shoulder.

He set Kate down on the table and they proceeded to tell her everything they had discovered about the rustler from Abilene.

"So, you think those cattle I saw this morning are stolen?" she asked.

She took the news surprisingly well.

"I'm afraid so, but just as I promised, we'll head out to the east pasture and check that downed fence and the cows, just to be sure."

"Should we have Dell ride out and get Nate?"

"No!" All three men said in unison.

"Surely, you don't think Dell has anything to do with this? He's been at White Willow nearly as long as I have."

"Let's just keep it between us for now. At least until we know what we're up against," Noah said.

"Levi and I will ride out with you. If it's rustlers we're dealing with, then it is under my jurisdiction too," Eamon assured Kate.

"We need to get out there before it gets too dark." The smell of snow lingered in the air and Noah wanted to make sure they would get back before it hit.

"Let's go."

CHAPTER THIRTEEN

The sky darkened to a smoky grey with thick clouds hanging low above the ranch. Noah tossed numerous blankets into the back of the wagon, along with several boards for mending the downed fence. The air had grown chilly and Kate pulled her coat up tighter against the knit scarf her mother had made for her years ago.

Noah climbed up onto the seat next to her and plopped one of her father's old hats on top of her head. "Are you sure you still want to come? It could be dangerous."

"I can't just sit here and wait, not knowing. I'd rather be with you. Dangerous or not." Kate pushed the hat up off her forehead. It was much too large, but she figured it would offer some protection if the snow started to fall before they returned.

"Thank you."

"You're a good woman, Katie Callahan," Noah said, picking up the reins. "Hi-yah!"

The ride out to the east pasture didn't take long, but as they approached the section where she'd seen the downed fence, Eamon and Levi circled back to them and dismounted, tying their horses to fence posts.

"Smoke." Levi said as he pointed to a stream of white vapors rising from the building next to the full corral.

Noah stopped the wagon, handed her the reins, then leaned over and kissed her fully on the mouth. When he pulled away, he looked down into her eyes. "If you hear shots, you ride out to Boswell's as quickly as you can and tell him everything, ya hear?" He looked at her, the corners of his fierce blue eyes crinkling as his stare deepened. "Promise me."

"How can you ask that of me?" Kate shook her head. "How can you ask me to leave you?"

"I have to know you're safe," he pleaded. "I can't lose you. Not now. Not ever." His jaw flexed. "Promise me!" he demanded, his eyes holding her hostage.

She stared at him without answering for as long as she dared.

"I promise," she finally relented.

He pulled her tightly into him, his hand holding her head against his shoulder. When he let go, he turned to leave without a word.

"Noah," she called, sliding toward the edge of the seat.

He looked back. Without another moment's hesitation, she reached out and grabbed a hold of his collar, pulling his face toward her and kissing him with fervor.

"Be safe!" she made her own demand in a whisper, pulling just far enough away that their lips were not fully connected. Her eyes opened, searching his for a promise.

Noah nodded and kissed her quick one more time. He jumped down from the buckboard and grabbed the rifle out of the holster at the side of the seat.

"I like doing that," he said as he handed the gun up to her and winked.

Kate tucked her face into her scarf and smiled. She loved that man. Why hadn't she just told him? The thought of their kiss warmed her on the inside and she raised her fingers to caress the vacant spot where his lips had just left hers. The chill of the open air brushed against her face and she shivered off the cold.

CRACK!

Kate's heart skipped a beat as she watched all three men she'd come with dive to the ground for cover as the shot ricocheted off the ground only a few feet from where Noah had landed. The horses pranced about, pulling the wagon back and forth as they sensed the newfound danger.

"Whoa," she called, attempting to calm them as she scanned the area, looking for where the shot had originated. There was nothing but open space between her and the cabin, nowhere for the men to take cover.

Promise me! Noah's voice echoed in her mind.

She slapped the reins to turn the wagon around toward Boswell's place when another shot rang out through the air. This time, movement in the trees above caught her attention. Fear gripped her chest as she glanced back over her shoulder. They would never be able to see their attacker's position from their locations on the ground and would be easy targets.

"Sorry, Noah," she said aloud before coming around full-circle and riding toward the men.

Kate scrunched down as far as she could in front of the seat and still be able to lead the horses. She wished she'd thought to wear her britches instead of the blamed skirt she had on. It would have made maneuvering so much easier.

When she reached Noah, she climbed down the backside of the seat, away from the shots, until her good foot hit the ground. Then, she lifted her rifle, steadying it against the wood, and fired two shots consecutively into the mountainside to create a distraction enough for the others to get to safety.

Noah, Levi, and Eamon all scrambled from the ground and ducked behind the wagon, each attempting to catch his breath.

"He's in the trees," Kate informed them, indicating the cluster on the mountainside where she'd seen movement.

"I'll get the horses," Levi said, nodding to his and Eamon's mounts.

"You can't be serious?" she asked incredulously. He would be completely unprotected.

When Levi looked at Noah and nodded in a slow deliberate fashion, both Noah and Eamon twisted forward against the wagon, bracing their arms against the wood and taking aim. They took turns firing shots and reloading while Levi ran out across the open land toward the restless horses.

CRACK! The shot pinged off of a piece of metal that shook the whole wagon.

Noah grunted next to her and she glanced over to see his jaw pulsating as he clenched his teeth together.

Eamon's gun clicked with an empty chamber and Noah wasn't yet ready to fire, so Kate slid the rifle back into the little groove she'd discovered in the edge of the wagon's board and aimed.

CRACK!

Kate ducked back down and watched with baited breath, her back up against the wagon, as Levi mounted the palomino he'd chosen in place of his own, the reins of Eamon's buckskin still in his hand. He laid close to the horse's neck as he made his way back to them. Instead of dismounting, he threw the reins to Eamon, who pulled himself up onto the back of his horse, his head low, and turned back to Noah.

"Near as I can tell, there's only one shooter," he said, as his mount pranced around excitedly. "We'll head up after him. You get that pretty little lady of yours to that shelter." He looked up as huge, white flakes of snow started to fall. "Looks like he's got a right cozy fire going inside."

"Eamon!" Levi called.

The Pinkerton tipped his hat at Kate and turned to follow Levi.

It took a moment, but she realized that the shooting had stopped.

"He's on the move," Noah said, sidling around her to the front of the wagon.

"What are you doing?" she asked in a whisper, though she didn't know why.

He climbed up onto the seat and reached down for her, swinging her up alongside him, crying out with pain. He slapped the reins and quickly closed the distance between them and the cabin.

"What's wrong?" she asked, looking him over as well as she could, blinking away the flakes that landed on her lashes.

"I'm fine," he said, his voice strained and grumbly.

The snow came down thicker now, making it difficult to see in any direction.

She'd lost sight of Levi and Eamon.

Noah jumped down off the buckboard and tethered the wagon team to the hitching post there. He took the rifle from her, set it on the edge of the wagon, and reached up for her, a grimace contorting his face.

Kate's eyes were drawn to the torn fabric and growingly red material of Noah's sleeve.

"You've been hit."

"It's nothing," Noah said, wrapping his hands around her waist and lowering her to the ground. "We have to get inside."

Click. There was no mistaking the sound of a gun's cocking hammer.

Noah froze, his eyes fixed on hers, warning her not to move, his body creating the perfect barrier between her and their foe.

"Drop it, Deardon, and step away from the wagon."

Kate's heart sunk. She knew that voice.

Dell.

CHAPTER FOURTEEN

How in blazes did he get down the mountain so fast?

Noah tossed his pistol onto the ground into the fresh blanket of snow that grew thicker by the second, and raised his hands shoulder level, his arm throbbing. Luckily, the bullet had gone straight through the fleshy part of his arm, but he'd lost a significant amount of blood. If he didn't tend to it soon…well, he didn't want to think about that. He needed to be strong. For her.

"Don't move," he mouthed to Kate as he slowly turned around.

"Nobody has to get hurt," the tall, older foreman said. "I'm just going to collect the cattle from the corral and we'll be on our way."

"You know I can't let you do that. It would ruin White Willow if anyone learned we'd been passing stolen cattle."

"And just what are you going to do to stop me?" Dell asked with a haughty chuckle. "I'm the one with the gun."

A whirling wind kicked up, blowing the dense snowflakes around in a dizzying flurry.

"Come on, Dell. You're smarter than this. You're not

going to make it very far in this storm. Think about it. There's nowhere to run." Noah was practically screaming to be heard above the sound of the mounting blizzard.

"Don't you worry none about me. We've got it all worked out."

"Dell," Kate stepped out from behind him.

Noah closed his eyes, looking heavenward.

Does she never do what she's told?

"I'm sorry it had to come to this, Katie." Dell grabbed her by the arm, twisting her just out of Noah's reach, and lifting her against his hip, then he motioned to the door with the barrel of his revolver.

Reluctantly, Noah turned his back to the man and headed for the cabin's small entrance, scanning the ground and the building for anything he could use to his advantage.

Nothing. He lifted the latch on the door.

"Hold up," Dell said, just before Noah pushed it open. "Put your hands together behind your back there, Deardon. And don't do anything stupid."

With a great deal of effort, Noah complied, wincing at the throbbing pain in his injured arm. He blinked back the unwitting tears that had formulated in his eyes and glanced back over his shoulder to try to catch a glimpse of Kate. Dell had her pinned up against the rough bark of the cabin's exterior wall as he wrapped the rope around Noah's wrists, the rough threads cutting into his flesh.

"Got yourself shot there, Deardon. Looks like a nasty wound. I'm sorry it's gone this far, but you left us no choice."

There it was again—the words 'we,' 'us.' Dell was not working alone. How many were there?

Kate cried out in a pain as the older man yanked her around, kicked the door open wider, and shoved them both inside the warmth of the little one-roomed cabin.

"You son of a—" Noah jerked his arms, but to no avail. He grew weaker by the minute and stumbled to the floor next to a ladder leading up to a small loft.

"Calm yourself there, Deardon." Dell laughed. "It would be such a shame if this gun were to go off in such close proximity to Miss Callahan."

Noah stopped struggling. Dell shoved Kate to the ground on the opposite side of him and bound her hands to his, then secured both of them to the bottom rung of the ladder. Her touch, however minute, gave him hope that they would both get out of this alive.

"Dell, please," she pleaded. "Don't do this."

"I'm afraid there is nothing any of us can do to stop it now." The old rustler grabbed a large leather pouch down from a hook near the fireplace and tin clanked against metal as he haphazardly began throwing several items from around the cabin inside it. He knelt down next to a wooden box in the corner of the room and pulled out a good-sized canvas bag bulging with what Noah suspected were coins. Maybe a payroll. Dell got to his feet and added the money to his pouch.

"What happened to Cliff, Dell?"

The foreman looked into the fire. "He got thrown from his horse. Happens all the time." His voice was distant, eerie as he spoke. He looked away from the flames and reached down to a bucket of water that had been sitting at the edge of the hearth.

The fire hissed angrily as he doused the flames, soaking the coals.

At least he didn't start the place on fire.

Kate's hands moved frantically as she stretched and twisted, trying to free herself from the ropes. If she didn't stop struggling, she would wear her wrists raw. He needed to get the knife out of his boot before she did any real damage.

"It wasn't an accident, Dell." Noah's focus was beginning to diminish and he shook his head in attempt to return clarity. "I saw the burrs. An experienced cowpoke like Thomas would have never saddled his prized Arabian with briars under the blanket. Tell me what happened." While their captor looked the other direction, Noah bent his leg up behind him.

"What makes you think I know anything about that?" Dell picked up a coat from the back of the lone chair in the room. He shoved his arms through the sleeves and slung the pouch across his shoulders.

"Dell," Kate said quietly. "Why are you doing this? You were like family to me and my da."

Noah could hear the pain in her voice and he wanted to just take her into his arms and soothe away her sorrows and her fears.

"Katie, I..."

A strong gust of wind blew the door open, knocking Dell forward and to his knees. The blizzard raged outside, storming the cabin with unrelenting ferocity. He bent over, grabbing the back of his head. When he slid his hands down, off his head, they were covered in blood.

"Dad blame it," he cursed, grabbing an old rag from the edge of rusted wash basin and held it over his wound. "I have to go."

"Dell, don't!" Noah warned. "You're hurt."

"This ain't nothing. You don't know him like I do."

"You'll die out there."

The foreman stopped, his hand holding onto the edge of the open door. "You don't get it, do ya, Deardon? They hang men like me."

"I'll talk to Nate," Kate pled loudly. "Reason with him."

"I can't be late." Dell trod outside, pulling the door shut behind him.

"What is he doing, Noah? We have to stop him. He'll die."

"Kate," Noah called her name, "we have to get out of these ropes."

"I've tried," she said. "Dell's a cattle man. He knows how to tie a knot."

"Kate," he tried again, bending his knee even farther to get his boot as close to their hands as possible.

"What?"

"My knife…" Noah fought the weariness that threatened to overtake him. "I can't…reach…"

"Noah?" Kate's voice sounded distorted and low.

He couldn't hold on any longer.

"Noah?"

Blackness surrounded him.

CHAPTER FIFTEEN

His boot.

From the awkward position he'd placed his leg, she figured that had to be where he kept his knife. Kate strained against the ropes in an attempt to reach his foot.

"Noah Deardon, don't you dare die on me!" she yelled, yanking on his hands, trying to wake him. He didn't stir and panic creeped in, squeezing her chest, her breaths labored and coming more rapidly.

This is not happening. I will not lose him. Not now.

Kate had never been sure she would ever be able to love again. Everyone she loved died and she did not want to face that heartache again. She bowed her head.

"Please, God," she pleaded, "don't take him from me."

She sat there a moment in the stillness, not sure what she was waiting for, but somehow took comfort in the silence. Within a few minutes, the disquiet in her heart slowed and a calming peace washed over her. With a new resolve, she jerked her hands against the ladder rung and the whole ladder slid— just an inch, but it moved.

"Just a little farther, Kate!" she told herself. "Come on."
She stretched again, her fingers lightly brushing the denim
material of Noah's trousers.

He slumped over awkwardly, his leg still twisted behind
him at an odd angle. She took a deep breath, bracing herself
for the pain she knew would ensue, and wrenched their hands
against their wooden jailor. It gave just enough that she
reached the hem of Noah's trousers and slid her hands up his
boot until she found the knife. Her fingers closed around the
hilt and she pulled it free.

Without wasting any time, she worked at the section of
rope that bound them to the ladder. Surprised by how quickly
the blade sliced through the ropes, she breathed in and then
out, slowing down enough that she wouldn't end up cutting
off their hands. She arranged the knife so that the metal edge
leaned up against the rope between her own hands and gently
moved it up and down until the bindings fell away from her
wrists.

Relieved, she quickly turned around, and cut the cords
restraining Noah, then readjusted his legs to lie out straight in
front of him. She dropped down to him, placing her ear on his
chest, watching his mouth for any indication he was still alive.
His breathing was slow and staggered.

She closed her eyes in gratitude. "Thank you."

She sprung upward, lifted her skirt, and cut several strips
of material from her petticoat to bind the wound on his arm.

With the storm still raging outside, the room grew darker
by the minute, making it nearly impossible to see him properly.
Kate had to think fast. She couldn't tell if he was still bleeding
or even where the shot had penetrated exactly, so she felt for
the hole in his shirt and tied one of the strips around his arm
just above that location. It would have to do until she had a
little more light in the room.

She'd noticed a stack of firewood in the corner of the
room when they'd first entered the cabin, so she stood up,

making her way there, and collected a few pieces, carrying them over to the fireplace where steam still rose from the center.

Even though Dell had doused the flames, some of the embers still glowed with heat, so she carefully arranged the logs the way her father had taught her when they'd first moved out to Laramie. She glanced around for anything she could use as kindling to reignite the fire. A small stack of disheveled papers caught her eye and she reached over and grabbed one from the top, but just as she started squeezing it together to be twisted into kindling, she thought better of it. There was a good chance that those papers contained some answers.

There was no time to inspect the documents further, but she couldn't burn any of them without knowing their contents. She set the paper back on the top of the stack so she could take a look at it later, after she'd seen to Noah and a fire. Before thinking any more about it, she ripped the petticoat from beneath her skirt and made quick work of tearing it into several pieces that could be used to incite new flames.

The material caught fire even faster than she'd expected and she once again expressed her gratitude. With the additional light from the hearth, Kate cut away the damaged material of Noah's sleeve and saw that the bleeding had already started to clot. She thought back to a few years ago when her brother had stepped on a sharp metal rod that had gone straight through his foot. Her mother had scrubbed it with soap and water, then doused it in vinegar to help prevent infection.

Kate scoured the little cabin, finding several jars of foodstuffs, but no vinegar. When she opened the cabinet beneath the makeshift bed, she discovered several bottles of various liquors and figured they had to be as strong as vinegar, if not more so. She grabbed a piece of her torn petticoat and opened one of the bottles, soaking the rag thoroughly.

The room warmed faster than she had expected and she wiped the perspiration from her brow as she scrubbed off what seemed like layers of both fresh and dried blood from Noah's unexpectedly sculpted arm. Her mouth went dry as she touched his hot skin, the heat in her cheeks not coming from the fire.

He moaned quietly, but didn't stir.

She shook her head and returned to her task.

Once she'd cleaned the sticky fluid from around the wound and could see the ridges of the hole properly, it started to bleed again, but only minimally. She placed a bowl under his arm and poured the remaining contents of the brandy bottle over the wound, then bound it with several clean cloths.

Luckily, it appeared that someone had been living in this small cabin, unbeknownst to her, for some time and it was well stocked. There were various food supplies as well as an unusually large stack of blankets, a single chair, small table, and plenty of wood for the fire. If they were going to be stuck here for any length of time, at least they wouldn't be starving or freezing.

Dell had been staying at the bunkhouse with the others, so Kate wondered who else may have been staying here and if he would be returning. She shook her head, refusing to let fear stop her from doing what needed to be done and right now, she needed water for Noah. So, she picked up the bucket and limped to the door. When she opened it, snow still fell, but the roaring wind had died down to a breeze and the sun—though it was setting—could be seen through the storm clouds.

Thank heaven for small mercies. And big ones.

She bent down and scooped snow into her bucket from the three foot high drift that had been blown up against the door, then secured the latch behind her and hung the container on the hook in the fireplace.

Cold air slipped through the cracks in the door, so Kate kicked the old, dusty braided rug up against the opening at the bottom of the door and stuffed the space between the hinges with a sheet that had been tossed over the corner of the bed.

She looked down at her patient lying on the floor. There was no way she would be able to lift a man Noah's size up onto the straw-filled mattress that topped the bed scrunched into the corner of the room, so Kate grabbed an armful of blankets from the shelf above a closet with its doors hanging off its hinges, and prepared a makeshift bed on the ground.

Once the chilly floor was adequately covered, Kate knelt down to the side of Noah and attempted to roll him over onto the blankets. It wasn't quite as simple as she'd thought it would be, and she spent the next several minutes trying to get him situated when he finally stirred enough that he rolled himself over and onto the warmth of the blankets.

Whew.

Kate rolled up a quilt to place beneath his knees, a smaller one for his head, then she tucked a coverlet up around his shoulders and neck, so he would stay warm. She'd done all she could think of to help him. Now, she'd just have to wait. And waiting had never been one of her strong suits.

Before long, she had a nice broth simmering over the fire and Noah appeared to be resting peacefully. If he didn't wake soon, though…

Stop it, Katie Callahan. He's going to be fine. He has to be.

CHAPTER SIXTEEN

Noah awoke to little paws kneading his chest. A loud purr pulled him from his cumbersome dreams, and he opened one eye to inspect the small, white and fawn-colored fluffy ball of fur nuzzling into his warmth. His hand rested in a curved position against his ear and face where the kitty had taken to suckling his fingertips.

"Where did you come from, little one?" he spoke to the wide-eyed kitten that had seen fit to snuggle up against him. He randomly thought of how much his nephews, Max and Gil, and even little Owen, would have loved having a little kitten to feed and play with back home, but doubted Emma would appreciate it much.

Noah blinked a few times, the reality of what had happened last night striking him with a force that nearly knocked him from the bed and he tried to sit up. Bad idea. The whole cabin seemed to swirl around inside his weighted head and darkness threatened the perimeter of his vision. He lay back down, forcing himself to focus on a single log in the rafters, and within a matter of moments, the crisp clarity of morning returned.

The kitten burrowed his head beneath Noah's hands, which now rested on his chest. There was no way such a young one could have survived the storm and he wondered where the animal had been hiding that would have muffled his surprisingly vocal ramblings.

"Where's your mama?" he asked in a voice higher pitched than usual.

"Meow," the kitten spoke loudly as if in response, confirming Noah's suspicion that he was hungry.

He waited a few more minutes until the grogginess had passed and propped himself up on his elbows, his arm stiff and achy. He scratched the kitten's head and laughed as the baby cat nudged his face with its nose.

"I'm trying," Noah laughed softly, basking in the light that came through the small window.

The storm had lifted, that much was apparent. A light chill blanketed the cabin and he glanced at the hearth still aglow with little red and orange cinders. They were safe. For the moment.

Kate.

The thought of his soon-to-be bride, pushed him up. He gritted his teeth as he held the kitty close to his chest, careful not to crush the fragile little thing. Kate must have been up most of the night, keeping the fire warm, and watching over him.

He found her sitting up against the wall, her legs straight out in front of her on the bed in the corner, with a blanket wrapped up around her shoulders, her eyes closed. She'd been brave. And she'd even shown kindness to a man undeserving of her compassion.

"I'm a very lucky man," he whispered into the air.

The sunlight played with the golden highlights in the otherwise dark waves of Kate's hair, creating an ethereal glow about her. She was simply breathtaking—easily the most beautiful sight he had ever lain eyes on.

Lord, thank you for getting us through the night.

Noah didn't know what the day would hold for them, but he knew they would face it together.

As he rolled off the makeshift mattress, he was amazed at Kate's resourcefulness. Not only had she managed to bandage his arm, but somehow, she'd gotten the blankets beneath him. She'd saved his life—there was no doubt. Now, it was his turn to take care of her. He set the kitten down on the ground and the little thing darted from one section of the enclosed room to the other, exploring.

Noah laughed as he walked over to the bed, placed his hand behind her head, and gently guided her down to the mattress. She opened her eyes, one at a time, and smiled.

"You are a sight for sore eyes," she said, tiredly.

He leaned down and placed a light kiss on her lips. He couldn't help himself.

"Thank you," he said in a whisper, and forced himself away from her. "Get some rest. I don't know how long we'll have to stay out here. We'll never be able to tread back in the snow with you still limping on that foot."

Unsure of what he would find outside, he grabbed one of the blankets and draped it around his shoulders before opening the door. Why he'd neglected to put on his coat before the drive up here was beyond him. It was probably frozen solid in the back of the buckboard.

"Hopefully, Levi and Eamon will know where to look for us." Noah told her, smiling when he glanced at her and found that she had fallen back asleep.

Good.

He had to believe that his cousin and friend had made it back to the homestead safely and without incident. Rustlers rarely worked alone and if there were more of them out there, no one would be safe until they were caught.

His thoughts turned to the livestock. If the cattle were going to have any chance at surviving, he would need to get back down to the winter pastures with Virg and the other hands to shovel out as much snow as possible and spread out fresh hay for the Herefords to eat. At least they'd gotten several wind fences and snow barriers raised before the storm and he prayed that they'd been able to withstand the heavy snow that had fallen through the night.

Noah pulled open the door and pushed through the drift that had accumulated there. While the snowfall was nearly two feet deep, he was comforted that the storm had only lasted the better part of a few hours.

He made his way to the side of the cabin where he'd left the wagon and was relieved to see that Dell had at least unhitched the horses, leaving only the buckboard behind and giving them a fighting chance. Another carriage of sorts peeked out from behind the cabin, but he was in no condition to explore right now. Not in the deep snow.

The corral was empty and only scooped hills and vales in the snow gave any indication as to what direction they had gone. Westward. Toward town.

Noah guessed that another hour had passed by the time Kate opened her eyes. He'd found a roll of jerky strips wrapped in cheesecloth in a box on the hearth and a sack with several apples and a tin of tobacco under the table. Not that they'd have any use for the snuff.

He dragged the chair over to the edge of the bed and held out an apple and some of the jerky for her.

"I'm afraid it's nothing like what Fannie can cook up for you."

She snatched the fruit from his hand and bit into its crisp flesh.

It wasn't until then that he noticed her newly scabbed wrists, the skin red and angry. He reached out and took her hands in his in order to inspect them more closely, then he glanced up at her, scrunching his brows together in concern.

"We got free," she said with a simple shrug, still chewing

her bite of apple.

"That we did." He didn't let go of her hands, but held them up in front of his face. "Thank you," he said as he placed a kiss on one wrist. "You are an amazing woman, Kate Callahan." He kissed the other wrist.

She smiled softly and swallowed.

"Thank you," she replied, "for trusting me. For listening to me. For taking care of me and my blasted foot."

They both laughed.

"And, for…waiting." Her honey eyes met his, and she bit her lip.

Noah leaned forward, wanting desperately to taste again of her apple-laced lips. She closed her eyes expectantly.

The kitty jumped up onto the bed and into Kate's lap, startling her. She jumped backward, her eyes shooting open with surprise. When she saw the visitor, she placed a hand over her heart before reaching down and picking him up so that his face was parallel with hers.

"Who is this little thing?" she asked, her crinkled brow evidence she hadn't know the kitten had been there either.

"He must have found a way in when it started getting cold. I think he's warm enough though as he's been darting around the room all morning."

"Flash," Kate said with a nod. "He's like a little flash of lightning, striking when you least expect it."

They laughed again as Flash sniffed at the jerky in Noah's hand. He stood and coaxed the kitty away from Kate, setting him on the floor where he'd placed a small cup of water from the bucket.

"Noooaaaahhhh!"

"Kaaaaaaate!"

"Did you hear that?" Kate asked, inching to the edge of the bed and gingerly standing up.

Noah strode to the door, peeking out the small window before swinging it wide.

"It's Levi," he announced, turning back to look at her.

She limped across the room and joined him at the door.

He placed his arm at her waist, holding her close to him, and they both raised their hands high into the air and waved.

"We're in here!" he shouted, his hand cupping his mouth. Though, as he looked down at Kate's smiling face, he almost wished they hadn't been found so quickly.

Almost.

CHAPTER SEVENTEEN

"We found him on our way out this morning to look for the both of you." Levi motioned to the body wrapped in a sheet and strung over the back of Virg's horse. "His mount must've thrown him. He's got a large gash in the back of his head."

It all seemed like one long nightmare and Kate just wanted it to be over.

Noah recounted what had happened with Dell in the cabin, while cuddling a still sleeping Flash in the underside of the wool blanket wrapped around him.

"Who's the other one?" he asked, pointing with his nose at the other body strung over the back of Eamon's horse. "He our shooter?"

Levi lifted back the sheet and a white boater hat fell to the ground.

Gregory Stiles.

"We're not sure how he was involved, but there's no question he's the one who shot you," Levi said grimly.

Kate opened the blanket and pulled out the papers she'd snatched from the table before they'd left the cabin, handing them to Eamon.

"Maybe these will help."

The Pinkerton scanned several pieces of the parchment and then looked up at Kate. "Where did you get these?"

"They were in the cabin. I almost burned them."

"Good thing you didn't. Do you know what you have found here?" he asked, handing them to Noah.

Flash jumped down out of Noah's arms and scampered across the snow, dashing from one location to another until he ran up the stairs and perched himself on the cleared porch railing, watching the goings on.

"Looks like you found a furry little friend," Levi nudged Noah.

"He's quite a survivor," Noah said as he glanced to the paper's Kate had found. "I imagine he'll keep vermin out of the house."

Kate looked back at Eamon. "Something told me they were important, but I didn't get a chance to look at them."

"They are detailed plans, outlining several heists, rustling jobs, and…"

"The murder of your father," Noah said quietly as he turned the next page, reading intently.

She stared at him, his words not registering properly with her.

"I'm sorry? What about my father's murder?"

Noah looked up at her.

"It was Stiles, Kate. He's the one who killed your father. It looks like he, Dell, and Clifford Thomas were all working together."

Kate shook her head. It couldn't be. Dell would have never allowed anyone to…to…

"You must be mistaken. Marshal Long killed my father," she insisted. "For White Willow. Just like he killed so many others for their ranches." She wasn't sure who she was trying to convince more, herself or the others.

"The correspondence is all right here. Gregory Stiles was no businessman from back East. He's a cattle rustler and a thief. Been living up in that cabin a yours in the east pasture since your father died, waiting, scheming to get this land."

"But, why? Why did he want this land so badly? It's mostly just open range farmland and mountains." She loved her land, but would gladly have given it all up to have her father back.

"I'm sorry, Kate," Levi said, putting an arm around her shoulders.

All the pain, the anger, the sorrow came flooding back in one giant wave of emotion, and she turned into him, not wanting Noah or the others to see her cry. She wanted Mr. Deardon, no, *needed* him to believe she was strong.

"There's some sort of chart here that diagrams all of White Willow Ranch, in its entirety. Look at this."

Kate waited a moment, sure her eyes would be red and puffy. She sniffled, then, reluctantly, she pushed herself away from Levi to stand next to Noah and see what he was talking about.

He handed her a handkerchief and she wiped her eyes.

"If this schematic is correct, it looks like this land— especially the mountain areas are a wealth of natural commodities."

"No wonder they wanted it," Levi said, looking over Noah's shoulder.

"Besides," Eamon chimed in, "the ranch was a good front for the stolen cattle. No one would have questioned the beef from a well-respected rancher."

"Excuse me, Miss Callahan," Virg stepped up, hat in his hand. "I apologize for interruptin' ma'am, but there's something I think you need to see."

They followed the hired hand out to the barn. Several pathways had already been cleared between the buildings and Kate noticed a few large mounds of snow, nearly as tall as haystacks, in the pasture where a large section had been shoveled away from the ground. The towering open barn at the far edge of the biggest corral had also been cleared and a couple hundred head of cattle grazed on the hay someone had spread there.

"Virg?" she asked before he opened the oversized barn doors. "Did you do all that?" She pointed at the fields.

"I helped," he said as he swung the doors wide open.

Amidst the animals on either side, there in the middle of the barn lay Cal, his hands and feet tied together like a new calf going in for branding, his mouth bound with a cloth gag.

"Virg, why is Cal tied up?" Kate asked as she rushed forward to help the hand.

When she reached him, there was a piece of paper attached to his ropes that read in large, black letters, "RUSTLER."

Kate ripped the tag from him and turned it to show the others. She stepped back as the man struggled, shaking his head wildly, and attempting to speak. She reached down and untied the gag from behind his head.

"He's crazy, Miss Callahan. Don't believe a word he says."

"Who, Virg?" she asked, her brows crumpled.

"No, the new fella. Everett."

She looked back at Virg and the others. She hadn't hired anyone new since before her father died. The only extra sets of hands they'd had on the ranch were...

No. Couldn't be.

"Everett?" she asked. "*Mason* Everett?"

"I don't know," Cal spat, emphasizing each word. "He came into the bunkhouse last night, just as the storm was starting, and took charge like he owned the place. Now, will you get me out of these things?"

"Not just yet," Kate replied, daring a glance at Noah.

He watched her with a raised brow.

"You know this Everett fella?" Noah asked as she

returned to them.

How could she explain Mr. Everett to Noah? The letters? His intentions? She *had* told him about the man, but now that he was here, she didn't know what to say.

"No one wanted to work for a woman!" Cal called out, pulling Kate from her thoughts. "But *I* stayed, didn't I?"

Noah strode into the barn and dropped down onto his haunches. "Why does this Everett character think you're a rustler, Cal?"

"I ain't never stole nothin'."

"Cal?" Noah's voice held a warning.

The hired hand dropped his head. "I didn't steal from anyone, I swear, but I didn't stop it from happening either. Dell paid me to keep my mouth shut. So I did. When I saw his cattle roaming with the others this morning, I just tried to round them up, is all. I don't know how he knew. I swear."

"Where is this Everett now?" Noah asked.

"Still shoveling snow out of the pastures, I'd reckon. He's hell-bent on making sure those cows don't freeze to death. Now, please. I told you what you wanted. Let me go."

"We'll let the sheriff deal with you," Noah said, standing up.

Cal whimpered. "Please." His plea was no more than a whisper.

Kate closed the gap between them as quickly as she could, her foot still not allowing much pressure. "Mr. Deardon," she started, then put her hand on his arm and looked up at him. "Noah, we both know that Nate and his Vigilance Committee are out to make examples out of anyone they can. We need to let him go," she whispered the last sentence. "Please."

Noah ground his teeth together, she could see his jaw pulsating, but he nodded his agreement. She reached down, lifting the hem of Noah's trousers and retrieved the knife from the sheath in the top of his boot.

He sucked in a loud breath.

She smiled at his reaction to the touch of her fingertips as they grazed the skin of his calf.

"You can stay on here through the winter if you'd like," she spoke as she knelt down next to Cal.

In that moment, she realized that the actions of just one man could have prevented her father's death, if he'd just had the courage or the integrity to report Dell's wrongdoing. She took a deep breath and closed her eyes, looking inside of herself for the courage to do what was right.

"I forgive you, Cal," she said quietly, opening her eyes and slicing through the ropes like butter. "But if you want to stay on here, you'll have to prove yourself."

"Yes, ma'am."

"And, Cal…"

"Yes, ma'am?" he said, sitting up and rubbing his wrists.

"I can only employ people I trust."

"Yes, ma'am." Cal pushed himself to his feet and stretched, then he strode toward Noah, Levi, and Eamon, his head bowed, but he stopped just before leaving and turned back to her. "Thank you, Miss Callahan. I won't let you down."

Kate watched as he left the barn, feeling at peace with her decision. She spotted Virg standing behind Levi, twisting the hat in his hands.

"Virg." She waved him to her. "Is everything all right?"

"It will be," he answered, unable to meet her gaze. "You are a good woman, Miss Callahan, and I just wanted you to know that I am more proud today to work for you than ever before."

"Thank you, Virg," she responded, her hand reaching out and resting on his shoulder. "You know, there is a foreman position that just opened up. I don't suppose you'd be interested?"

She glanced back at Noah with a twinge of guilt that she hadn't consulted her soon-to-be husband before offering Virg the job. He simply raised a brow and came to stand next to her.

"Yes, ma'am. Thank you," the hired hand said, his face donning a smile as he reached out to shake her hand, then Noah's. He shoved the hat on his head. "Better not stand here jawing. There's still a lot of work that needs to be done." He hurried out of the barn, leaving just Levi, Eamon, her, and Noah.

"Will there ever be a time when those words aren't true?" she breathed the question, ending in a sigh and they all laughed.

"I'm sorry about your dad, Kate," Noah said, slipping his hand around hers and squeezing.

She leaned into him, enjoying how well she fit below his arm.

"Me too."

"Well, we've got a train to catch tonight," Levi stated with a clap of his hands. "That is, if they've been able to clear the snow and attach the plow to the cowcatcher."

"We'll miss you around here," Kate said, stepping forward and putting her arms around Levi. "What time is the train supposed to leave?" she asked as she released him.

"Six o'clock. I hate to leave you all with everything that just happened, but I'm afraid my responsibilities lie elsewhere."

"I heard you were looking for me."

All heads turned to look to where the voice had come from. A tall, dark-haired man with ice-blue eyes and a muscular physique stepped into the doorway, sticking his shovel into the ground.

"I'm Mason Everett."

Oh, my!

"Everett." Noah's head bobbed up and down as he did a quick sizing up of the man. "Ahhh, the mysterious new cowpoke. I understand we have you to thank for securing the cattle last night and helping to clear out much of the snow this morning." He extended his hand. "I'm Noah. Deardon."

"Deardon?" Mr. Everett asked with a little tilt of his head.

"You're not any relation to Lucas Deardon from Montana?"

"He's my little brother." Noah nodded proudly. "You know Lucas?"

Kate hadn't heard a lot about Noah's family and talk of his brother piqued her interest.

"Yes, sir!" Mr. Everett said enthusiastically. "Just came from Whisper Ridge where I've been working as foreman for the last few years."

She watched the exchange with curiosity and trepidation.

"What brings you out this way? You're lucky you made it before that storm hit. Travelling that kind of distance in the winter is either mighty brave or mighty stupid."

"Yes, sir. I thought the reward would be well worth the risk."

Kate took a deep breath and bit her lip. She needed to be the one to tell Noah, not Mr. Everett. When the fine-looking stranger's eyes found hers, heat filled her face at the appraising smile that touched his features.

"And what reward might that be?" Noah asked nonchalantly.

"I've come to marr—"

"Hello, Mr. Everett," Kate said, stepping forward. "I'm Kate."

The man practically knocked the hat from his head, pulled off his gloves, and extended his hand with a slight bow. "Miss Callahan," he said warmly. "You are even prettier than I'd imagined."

"Thank you," she said with an uneasy smile. "So are you."

Heat flooded her cheeks at the admission.

Despite the chilly morning, the air around her seemed a bit stifling as all eyes fell on her.

"Noah," she turned to him and took a deep breath before continuing. "Mr. Everett is here…"

Just say it.

Yes?" Noah said, waiting, one brow raised.

"…in answer to my ad." The rest of the sentence spilled out of her mouth faster than she knew herself capable. Then, she folded her lips together, wary of his response.

Noah threw his head back and laughed heartily.

"Is that what's gotten you all nervous and acting so strangely all of the sudden?" He turned to the mail-order-suitor. "I came for the same reason, Everett. She's quite a catch."

The man's smile faltered.

"Mr. Everett, I can't tell you how much I have enjoyed your letters. I looked forward to them every week."

"As did I, Miss Callahan," he responded, switching his glance back and forth between her and Noah. "I've thought about this day longer than I care to admit." He settled on looking at her. "I guess I was just too enamored to realize that others would see in you what I have and that they would call on you as well."

Tell him, Kate.

"I know you've come all this way…"

He dropped his head.

"But, you've already made your choice," he finished for her, nodding, his lips puckered with realization as he looked down and kicked at some imaginary pebble on the ground.

"Yes."

"Well, that's that then." He knocked his gloves against the leg of his denims.

"I'm sorry. I…"

"No need for apologies, ma'am. If there is one thing I've learned about Deardons, it is that you don't bet against them. If he's anything like his brother," he said with a half-hearted smile, "then he's good stock." He held out his hand again to Noah. "You're a lucky man, Deardon."

Noah returned the gesture, then slipped his hand over Kate's.

"Don't I know it."

CHAPTER EIGHTEEN

The savory aroma of Fannie's chili cooking on the stove was enough to send Noah's grumbling stomach into fits. The cook had made a thick, buttery cornbread and apple dumplings to serve along with it, but they wouldn't be ready to eat for another half an hour.

"It's been a while since I've eaten a home cooked meal," Mason said. "Thank you for inviting me to stay."

Somehow, Noah had found himself alone on the porch with the man who'd come to Laramie with hopes of marrying his Kate and counted himself fortunate that he'd arrived first. He imagined that Everett had no lack of female attentions with his easy smile and good work ethic.

"You handled yourself pretty well out there, both with the cattle and with Kate. You've proven you've got a good head on your shoulders and that you aren't afraid of a little hard work. Or a lot. I thought you might consider staying on. At least through the winter." Noah looked at the man who'd endeared himself to Kate through his letters and was grateful for the kindness and encouragement he'd offered her during a difficult time. He leaned down, his elbows on his knees and his hands folded together in front of him.

"You're offering me a job?"

"If you want it." Noah nodded. "The way I figure it, if my brother trusted you, that's all I need to know. I believe you to be a man of your word. Besides, you were smart enough to figure out that Kate is worth fighting a Wyoming storm, and we could use a little of that kind of determination and perseverance around here. The job's yours if you want it."

"That's awfully generous of you, Mr. Deardon."

"Call me Noah."

"Noah, thank you. I would consider it an honor. I'll stay. At least until I figure out where to go from here."

Noah understood all too well the need to figure out what life had in store for a man's future and felt very blessed that his included one Kate Callahan.

"Great. Now, if you'll excuse me for a moment. It's torture sitting right here with the smell of that delicious food floating through the cracks and not being able to eat. I've got a few things to attend to."

Mason stood and followed him down the porch stairs.

"I noticed the gate on the corral next to the barn is barely hanging on its hinges and thought I'd do something about that."

"They'll call when supper's ready." Noah laughed, tipping his hat at the man as he headed for the stable, but as he passed the bunkhouse, he noticed Levi inside. He pushed open the door.

He didn't know what to say. 'Thank you' just didn't seem like it was enough. If it hadn't been for Levi, he would never have risked everything for the chance to find his place in a little town like Laramie or to be with a woman as incredible, strong, and beautiful as Kate.

"I have something for you," he said, motioning out the door with a slight jerk of his head.

"I just finished up." Levi cinched up his bag and followed

him out to the stable.

"I offered Everett a job to stay on through the winter. I figured he was as good a ranch hand as I would find and he needed a place to stay, so it will work out."

He and Levi had been together for near a month and Noah was just beginning to realize just how much he was going to miss his cousin.

"There are still several towns along the transcontinental route that will need men like him. Don't be surprised if I lure him away from here with dreams of a place of his own—and maybe a woman to go with it."

They both laughed.

"Well, you were right. This trip to Wyoming is exactly what I needed. Kate is amazing." Noah paused at Apollo's stall gate and reached down into the bag of apples. "I can't thank you enough for dragging me out here. I could have missed out on life without my other half."

"Now, you're just getting sappy," Levi called it like it was.

"He's yours."

"What are you talking about?"

"You cannot keep riding that little pony of yours across the west. You need a dependable mount that you can trust. I'm giving you Apollo."

"And what are you going to do?"

"I did train horses for the first twenty years of my life, I think I'll be okay."

The light-colored Arabian perked his head up and over the stall gate.

Noah laughed. "I'm going to train this one," he said, rubbing the horse's nose and neck. "Ares. It's quite fitting, don't you think. A lover and a fighter."

"What is it with you and the Greek gods?" Levi asked, shaking his head as he strode over to Apollo and brushed his hands across his neck and back. "Thank you, Noah. For Apollo, and for taking a chance—even at great risk. You were the right man for this place. And for Kate."

"And she is the right person for me. I'd like to do something special for her. Will you help?"

"Of course. What can I do?"

CHAPTER NINETEEN

It had been a long time since Kate had taken a bath, let alone in the middle of the day, but Noah had insisted on carrying several buckets of steaming water into one of the back rooms and filling the oversized washbasin he'd purchased in town. She dipped down into the warm, sudsy water, luxuriating in the feel of it on her skin, and allowing it to wash away her cares.

"Miss Kate," Fannie said, peeking around the door as she came into the room with a towel and a clean dress ensemble. "I thought you might like some help brushing your hair. You've had a hard couple of days and it's the least I can do." She hung a pretty rose colored skirt and lighter pink blouse over the back of the quilt rack, along with all of the accompanying undergarments.

Kate thought of telling her just to bring in the old pair of her brother's trousers and one of her father's button-down shirts, but thought better of it. Putting on something nice to wear would complete the experience. She doubted many women this far west would enjoy such luxuries as a warm bath in their own home.

Fannie dragged one of the high-backed chairs in the room over to the tub, sat down, and pulled the pins from Kate's hair, allowing it to drape down the back of the basin. The woman worked through the snarls without Kate wincing every couple of seconds in pain. Instead, the brisk movements of the brush sweeping through her hair and Fannie's constant twisting and pulling soothed her even more.

"Do you need anything else, my dear?" Fannie asked as she stepped toward the closed door.

"I have everything I need," she replied, soaking in the moment.

As the water started to cool, Kate bemoaned the end of her much needed indulgence and quickly washed up, then dressed. She glanced in the small, square mirror hanging on the wall next to the door, pleased with her elegant hairstyle and the pink glow to her cheeks.

She wanted to skip down to her room, but the ankle still pained her enough that she was just happy she could make the distance on her own.

After lacing up her boots as tightly as she could for support, and pulling on a fancy coat that had belonged to her mother, she gingerly stepped out onto the porch, awed by the spectacular sight of the hitched sleigh on the snow, and Noah standing in front of it wearing a dark grey suit and a tailored coat. She'd have never guessed he owned such elegant wear.

He took her breath away as he tipped his hat before leaping up the steps two at a time and sweeping her up into his arms.

"Noah Deardon, what on earth are you up to?" she asked with a playfully narrowed gaze.

"The day is so beautiful, I thought we could enjoy it on a ride into town." He carried her to the sleigh and set her down on the seat, then climbed up next to her.

After everything that had happened, physically and emotionally within the last twenty-four hours—not to mention the last couple of months, Kate decided a little time to recuperate was exactly what she needed, even if it was only for the day.

She looked down at Mr. Everett, who stood in the doorway of the stable, leaning with his hands on the shovel in front of him, and smiled. He'd been very gracious. He would make another woman very happy someday.

Noah kept a slow, even pace with the horses on the way into town. The biting chill from the previous night had turned into a mildly cool, winter's afternoon, but Kate nestled a little closer to the handsome man sitting next to her all the same. The sun occasionally showed its rays as it shot through the clouds hovering across the sky, adding depth and beauty to the landscape.

When they arrived in Laramie, Noah drove straight to the little brown church at the far edge of town, which sat in contrast amongst the neighboring bawdy saloons. Kate looked up at Noah and he turned on the seat, holding her hands in his.

"Kate," he said, searching her eyes, "I want to marry you."

"Me too," she nodded enthusiastically.

"I know you wanted to wait until the Harvest Jubilee to make it official, but I don't want to wait that long. I love you, Kate Callahan. Will you marry me? Today?"

She didn't need time to think, only to voice her answer.

"Yes," she replied. "Oh, yes." The hole that had been empty inside of her for so long, spilled over with the love she had for this man. He was her everything and she couldn't wait to be his wife.

Noah jumped down from the sleigh and held up his hands for her. Her heart beat excitedly, but she wasn't scared. Or nervous. It felt right and she knew that with him by her side, no matter where they were, she would always be home.

Noah helped her up the steps to the chapel to find Cindy and her husband, Reverend Jones, standing at the front of the room, with Levi and Eamon to the side. She'd never believed that she would ever be this happy, but she couldn't imagine her life without this man who'd slipped into her heart unannounced and made her complete.

She wasn't sure how it happened all so quickly, but the good reverend pronounced them man and wife.

"You may now seal this union with a kiss."

Noah took her into his arms.

"You *are* a good woman, Katie Callahan Deardon," he said, closing the short distance between them in a tender melding of their lips. "*My* woman. My wonderful, beautiful bride. I am yours. Forever."

"I will never tire of hearing that," she said, snuggling into him. "You are my irresistibly strapping and hard-working husband, and I am all yours. Forever."

THE END

To read more about Noah's brothers,
check out the rest of the Deardon Mini-Series
—and—
To read more about his cousin, Levi Redbourne,
check out the Redbourne Series

Also by KELLI ANN MORGAN

JONAH
DEARDON MINI-SERIES, BOOK ONE

LUCAS
DEARDON MINI-SERIES, BOOK TWO

THE RANCHER
REDBOURNE SERIES BOOK ONE
COLE'S STORY

THE BOUNTY HUNTER
REDBOURNE SERIES BOOK TWO
RAFE'S STORY

THE BLACKSMITH
REDBOURNE SERIES BOOK THREE
ETHAN'S STORY

THE IRON HORSEMAN
REDBOURNE SERIES BOOK FOUR
LEVI'S STORY

Available from INSPIRE BOOKS

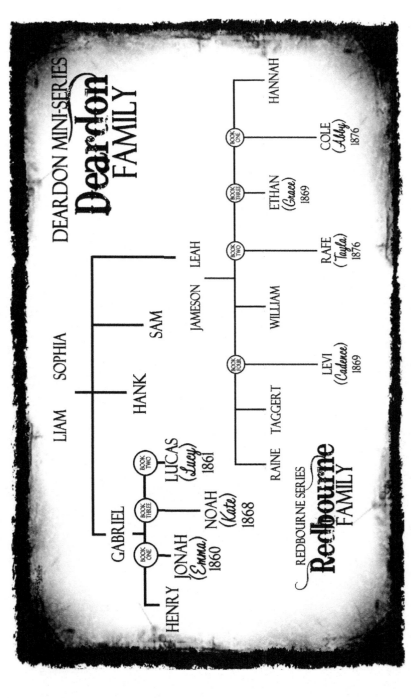

ABOUT THE AUTHOR

KELLI ANN MORGAN recognized a passion for writing at a very young age. Since that time, she has devoted herself to creativity of all sorts—moonlighting as a cover designer, photographer, jewelry designer, motivational speaker, and more.

She has been asked many times why she writes western historical romance novels and the answer is simple--she loves romance, chivalrous cowboys, horses, and the Old West. It is important to her that when her readers curl up with one of her books that he or she is transported into a wonderful world of adventure where good conquers evil and the hero gets the girl. Then, when the ride is over, she hopes you'll feel uplifted, satisfied, and ready for the next adventure. Her novels are on the sensual side of PG—without all the graphic love scenes.

FACEBOOK:
https://www.facebook.com/KelliAnnMorganAuthor

E-MAIL:
kelliann@kelliannmorgan.com

NEWSLETTER SIGN UP:
http://bit.ly/1iFvvwy

WATCH FOR

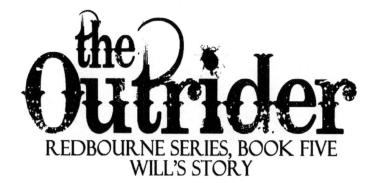

REDBOURNE SERIES, BOOK FIVE
WILL'S STORY

OTHER PG WESTERN READS
YOU MIGHT ENJOY...

KRISTIN HOLT
THE BRIDE LOTTERY

CAROLINE FYFFE
MONTANA DAWN

KIMBERLY KREY
CASSIE'S COWBOY CRAVE

BELLA BOWEN
GENEVIEVE

KIT MORGAN
AUGUST

DIANE DARCY
STEAL HIS HEART

Printed in Great Britain
by Amazon

53573824R00098